SENT *to* DEATH

A MEGAN MONTAIGNE MYSTERY

BOOKS by PAM STUCKY

FICTION

Mystery

Death at Glacier Lake
Final Chapter: A Megan Montaigne Mystery
A Conventional Murder: A Megan Montaigne Mystery
The Caramel Crow: A Megan Montaigne Mystery
Sent to Death: A Megan Montaigne Mystery

Balky Point Adventures (MG/YA sci-fi)

The Universes Inside the Lighthouse
The Secret of the Dark Galaxy Stone
The Planet of the Memory Thieves
The Perils of the Infinite Task

the Wishing Rock series (contemporary fiction) (novels with recipes)

Letters from Wishing Rock
The Wishing Rock Theory of Life
The Tides of Wishing Rock
From the Wishing Rock Kitchens: Recipes from the Series

NONFICTION

the Pam on the Map travel series (wit and wanderlust)

Pam on the Map: Iceland
Pam on the Map: Seattle Day Trips
Pam on the Map (Retrospective): Switzerland
Pam on the Map (Retrospective): Ireland

www.pamstucky.com

SENT *to* DEATH

A MEGAN MONTAIGNE MYSTERY

PAM STUCKY

Wishing Rock Press

Published in the United States by Wishing Rock Press.

Cover artwork by Madison Erin Mayfield
Cover design by Pam Stucky

ISBN (print): 978-1-940800-24-0
ISBN (ebook): 978-1-940800-25-7

www.wishingrockpress.com

for my fellow climbers

"Where death waits for us is uncertain; let us look for him everywhere."

— *Michel de Montaigne, 1533–1592*

MAP OF EMERSON FALLS

(subject to reconstruction)

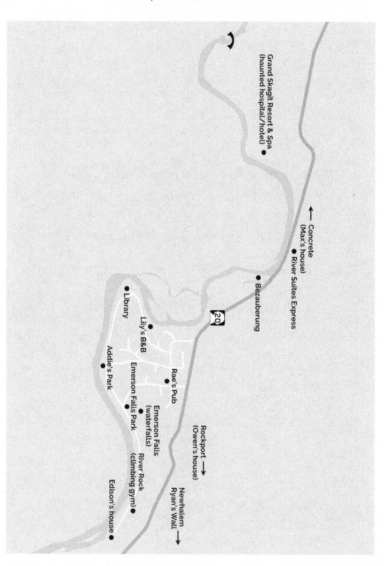

ONE

"They're not going to make us climb *that*, are they?" Megan Montaigne's eyes grew wide with terror as she gazed up at the towering outdoor rock climbing wall. The beige and gray three-story-high structure had been built to resemble an actual rock face, but all over it brightly colored rock climbing holds of various sizes and shapes were attached. Scattered over the surface, short ropes were attached with carabiners. The wall seemed impossibly vertical.

She shifted her glance to another climbing wall, this one even taller: maybe fifty feet high. Its dark charcoal gray face, baking in the bright summer sun, was smooth with a faint line down the middle from top to bottom delineating two separate sections on either side. Identical sets of holds had been placed in the exact same positions on each section, and two extremely long ropes cascaded down from their anchors at the top of the wall.

"Or *that*?" Megan said. "They know I'm not actually a rock climber, right? I'm a library director. We didn't learn this in school."

Megan's friend Lily Bell, who was also craning her neck to look up at the top of the wall, laughed. "A: They know you are not a rock climber. B: You're here to be an extra in a film, not a professional climber. They're not going to make you do anything that would kill you. At least, not unless you fill out a liability waiver first. C: No one is forcing you to do anything. Oh and D: You should try it. It's fun!" She punched Megan lightly, even delicately, on the shoulder.

Megan shook her head dubiously. "I don't know. Seems like the ground is a pretty solid place to be." She was dressed for the job she'd come for: workout gear, long dark hair pulled back in a ponytail. "Actors need motivation, right? I am not yet feeling my motivation." She tugged at her ponytail nervously.

Lily laughed. "You're not an actor. You're an extra. Don't be so nervous. They have so many safety precautions in place. I mean, it's possible to get hurt, but it's possible to get hurt walking on the street, too, right? Seriously, it's fun. Steve and I are getting memberships. And Edison is offering the B&B discounted day passes for our guests."

"Speaking of," said Megan, "is Edison here?"

Megan scanned the area, taking in the scene. The rock climbing gym built by their friend Edison Finley Wright was brand new, just barely opened, but already it was being put into use as a movie set for an independent filmmaker. On this sunny summer day, the space outside the gym was buzzing with people. Edison had bought up a good bit of land for the climbing gym, and the area was now dotted with trailers and busy-looking people milling around, talking into tiny walkie talkies clipped to their shirts, trying to get the not-busy-looking people organized. Megan's eyes landed on each person for a split second as she tried to find Edison—who was also previous owner of the mansion that had been turned into the library where she now worked and lived, and Emerson Falls' wealthiest resident.

"I don't see him. Maybe around the other side of the gym?" Megan said, and then she jumped out of her skin as a voice boomed from behind her.

"Megan!" said Edison, clapping a warm hand onto her back. "Lily! Isn't this exciting?"

Putting a hand to her chest to calm her startled heart, Megan turned toward the voice. She couldn't help but smile at the man's enthusiasm. Her heart fluttered again, but this time it was Edison. Something about him was simply electric. His piercing green-blue eyes were full of passion for life and his grin somehow flowed through his full body. Megan remembered he'd gone through a difficult divorce from an abusive woman a few years earlier. Seeing him so happy now filled her heart with joy.

"This gym is absolutely gorgeous," Megan said. She hadn't seen the man for months but conversation felt as easy as if they'd already been talking for hours. "At least from the outside. I haven't been inside yet. Although as I was telling Lily, don't expect me to be climbing any of these outside walls anytime soon." She smiled, nodding toward the swarms of film cast and crew. "Brand new and already you've made it into a hub of excitement. Wouldn't expect any less from you, Edison. I never asked you, what made you decide to build this? Here in little Emerson Falls?" She pointed at the exterior climbing walls, the gym itself.

"My daughter's in college," Edison said, his eyes traveling to the top of the tallest wall as if he could see her there. "I went and visited her for a couple of weeks last year. Climbing is her new passion, so we went to her gym a lot, and I fell in love with climbing, too. As it turns out, though, there aren't a lot of climbing gyms up in this part of Washington, out here in the North Cascades. Almost all of the indoor gyms are out west, closer in to Puget Sound. A real commute for a guy who wants to climb. In fact, there's not a climbing gym closer than forty miles from here. But I didn't want to give up climbing." He looked up at the shorter of the two outdoor walls with a smile of satisfaction and pride. "I decided to pump up the Emerson Falls economy a bit. Build a rock climbing gym, hire some people. Give the tourists another activity, another destination, another reason to come. I plan to work with the hotels, now that we have both River Suites and Remington's place, get everyone on board, everyone involved. Make it work for the whole community."

"The new Grand Skagit Resort and Spa," Megan said, nodding. "Also known as the former haunted hospital. That's great that you'll be working with the big hotels," she said, "but don't forget Emerson Falls' own favorite bed and breakfast." Lily was one of Megan's best friends, and there was no way she was going to let Edison leave her out of his plans.

"And there are plenty of other smaller rental places, too," Lily said, never one to hoard the spotlight. She tucked a strand of her shoulder-length auburn hair behind her ear.

"Of course," Edison said, turning his grin to Lily. "You are the pinnacle of hospitality. We won't forget you. It doesn't get any better than Lily's B&B. Anyway, this film opportunity came up unexpectedly. As we were planning and building the gym, I connected with a lot of climbers. One told me about this indie movie a friend of his was working on. We met and talked it over, and now here we are. It'll be great marketing for the gym and for Emerson Falls and for Remington's resort. Most of the cast and crew are staying there."

"Are they all climbers?" Megan asked. "The cast and crew."

"A lot of them are, yes," Edison said. His eyes raced around the scene and settled on a young man in loose, somewhat raggedy pants and a yellow T-shirt. "That's Brenden," he said, pointing. "The one in the yellow shirt. He tried out for one of the two main male parts, but he came in third. Some climbers call him Donut."

"Donut?" Lily said. "Why?"

Edison laughed. "His real name is Brenden Kogut."

Lily squinted. "I still don't get it. He's called Donut because …?"

"Because Kogut sounds like Donut," Edison said, as if it was the most obvious thing in the world.

Megan narrowed her eyes, trying to see it. "Hmm," she said.

Edison moved his attention to another man, maybe early twenties, almost startlingly handsome, wearing raggedy cargo pants and a gray T-shirt, standing with a confidence like he owned the gym himself. "That's Bee," he said. "Great climber. One of the two leads. Enzo Larrabee."

"Larrabee, thus Bee," Lily said. "That makes sense."

Edison scanned the crowd further and finally found what he was looking for. "That over there with the red T-shirt, that's Fox. Lead role. Amazing climber. He even has sponsorships. I've gone out climbing with him a few times. He's great."

"And he's called Fox because … he's sly and wily?" Lily asked.

"No, that's his name," Edison said. "Kendrick Fox." He winked at Lily. Lily shook her head, laughing.

"Hey!" Another booming voice and beaming face called out to Megan, Lily, and Edison. Max Coleman jogged the few paces between him and his friends, a backpack slung over his shoulder, his glistening, perfect white teeth and deep dimples heralding his arrival.

"Max!" Megan called out as he approached, returning his wide smile. The Deputy whose beat included Emerson Falls was one of her favorite people. "What are you doing here?"

"Same thing you are, I assume," he said, tilting his head toward the gym. "Extras. I've done some climbing in the past. Thought I'd dust off my old climbing shoes." He nodded at the backpack, which he set on the ground.

On hearing Max's voice, a woman standing just a few yards away from them turned and looked. She saw the Deputy and her jaw dropped open as she rushed toward him and straight into his arms. "Maaaaaaxxxx!" she said, hugging him energetically. "Max Coleman!"

Laughing, Max looked down at the woman, his brown eyes wrinkling at the corners as his grin grew even wider. "Piper Tuesday!" he said with disbelief. "Piper Tuesday! Look at you! Piper Tuesday!"

The woman pulled away from Max and twirled. "In the flesh! What are you doing here?" she said. She reached for Max's arm again, then slid her hand down into his, intertwining fingers as she clasped her other hand over the joined hands. From the way she was looking at him, it was clear they were, or had been, close.

"The film needed extras," Max said, shrugging. "I thought, why not?"

Megan thought Max seemed to be under a bit of a spell. He certainly wasn't pulling away from her intimate touch. Who was this woman?

"You still climb?" the woman asked. "Good for you!"

"I don't, actually," Max said. "But I still have my shoes." He pointed at his bag. He suddenly remembered there were other people standing with them. "Sorry, everyone! This is Piper. Piper Milan. Piper, this is Megan Montaigne, Lily Bell, Edison Wright."

"We've met," Edison said, nodding at Piper. "Good to see you."

"Nice to meet you," Megan said, holding out her hand. Piper took it in hers and shook it warmly, then returned her hands to Max's. "Piper Tuesday? Or Piper Milan?" Megan asked.

"Piper Tuesday Milan," Piper said. She looked at Max, pleased. "My middle name is Tuesday. 'Tuesday's child is full of grace,' and all that. My parents were hippies in their teens and hadn't quite recovered by the time I was born. Max always liked to call me Piper Tuesday."

Megan nodded. She could feel Lily's curiosity practically bursting out of her, and she hoped her own energy wasn't quite as obvious. If Max always referred to this woman affectionately by her first and middle name, clearly there was some history there.

Lily was not one to pry, but Megan was. She asked the question they all wanted the answer to. "How do you two know each other?"

Max opened his mouth to speak, but Piper beat him to it. "We dated. Years ago." She looked up at Max. "He dumped me and broke my heart."

Max blushed and looked down.

"It's okay," Piper said. "I've forgiven you." She winked.

"So what are you doing here?" Max asked. "Just happened through?"

"My boyfriend is in the movie," Piper said, finally untangling her hands from Max's. "The one in the red shirt over there." She waved at the man to get his attention, then made a wide scooping gesture to indicate he should join them. He nodded and started toward the group. "I'm in the movie, too, but just a small part," Piper continued as her boyfriend jogged over.

"Your boyfriend is Fox?" Megan said. "Kendrick Fox, right? Edison was just telling us he's a great climber."

Fox reached them just as Megan made the comment. He winked at Edison. "You're too kind," he said.

"Fox, this is Megan, Lily, and Max. Max and I go way back. He's the one who dumped me so I could find you." She wrapped her arm around her boyfriend's waist.

"Thanks, man," Fox said, chuckling lightly. "I owe you one." He draped a long, strong arm onto Piper's shoulders. "Your loss."

Megan noticed that Fox's smile now looked a bit forced. "Say, Edison," Max said without acknowledging Fox's comment. "Is there a bathroom somewhere?" He picked up his backpack.

Edison looked from Fox to Max. "Sure, follow me," Edison said, and he led Max away.

Megan saw Piper's gaze linger on Max as he walked with Edison toward the gym. There was a story there, and Megan would get it out of one of them, soon enough.

Then Megan noticed someone else watching them. The one Edison had called Bee. Enzo Larrabee. The other main actor. While Piper continued to watch Max, Bee's eyes were focused on Piper and Fox. The look on his face made Megan feel uncomfortable. What was it? Jealousy? Or something more? Anger?

She shifted her attention back to Piper and Fox. "Welcome to our little town," she said. "Hopefully you'll be comfortable here. I hear you're staying over at the haunted hotel!" She laughed.

Fox stiffened. He looked at Piper, one eyebrow raised. "At the what?" he said.

"The Grand Skagit Resort and Spa, right?" Megan said. Fox and Piper nodded, their attention piqued. Megan continued. "It was built on land where there used to be a haunted hospital. The developer renovated it but word on the street is that some of the ghost-guests haven't left."

Fox pulled his arm off Piper's shoulder and shook his head. "I'm not staying in a haunted hotel," he said. He glared in Piper's direction. "You can stay there but I'm not staying there."

Piper frowned. "It should be fine?" she said, looking to Megan for reassurance. "I mean ghosts aren't real, right?"

"No one has been killed by one of their ghosts yet," Megan said, sensing that even as she joked, she wasn't helping.

"That Ouija board incident I told you about from when I was a kid…" Fox said, his words focused at Piper, like he'd almost forgotten Megan and Lily were still there. He shuddered.

Piper bit her lip. "Is there somewhere else we could stay?"

Lily sighed. "Normally I'd offer you my place, a B&B, but we're full right now. There's the River Suites, near the resort, I'm sure they have room."

A lightbulb went off in Megan's head. She suddenly knew how she'd find out more about Piper and Max! "Orrrrrrr," she said, "I can offer you something even better. I live on the top floor of the library. It used to be a mansion that Edison owned, but he donated it to the county and it was converted for library use. The top floor is my apartment, plus some guest suites. It's on the river, it's closer to the gym here, the film site, than the resort or the other hotel. It's private, and no one is using the guest rooms right now. If you want to stay with me, you're more than welcome."

"And it's not haunted?" Fox said.

"One hundred percent not haunted," Megan said. "Although I wouldn't mind a friendly ghost downstairs in the library, just for character …" Megan saw Piper's glare and realized she was talking in the wrong direction. "But no, one hundred percent not haunted."

Piper looked at Fox, who was nodding with a look of resignation. "Definitely," she said. "That sounds amazing. Thank you!"

"No problem," Megan said. "I'm always happy to help." She glowed with satisfaction. She wasn't being nosy, she told herself. Just curious. As any human would be. And mighty generous, too, offering up her own home. After all, any friend of Max's was surely a friend of hers.

TWO

"So you're the extras Edison insisted on."

Megan had agreed to meet up with Piper and Fox at the end of the day to take them to the library and get them settled in the guest rooms. Then, she and Lily had asked who they should report to for the day. Piper had pointed to a petite, angular woman with short, angular, nearly black hair and dark, angular glasses. They made their way over and introduced themselves, only to be met with a very lukewarm reception.

The woman pursed her red-stained lips. "I'm Heather Birdsong, the Assistant Director for this film. I'll be in charge of you." She sighed heavily, as if she'd been assigned to babysit unruly sloths, and looked at her clipboard. "Isn't there supposed to be another one of you? A man?"

"Max?" Megan said. "Didn't he already check in with you?"

"Yes, I have Max, he's in wardrobe. A man named Scott."

Megan was puzzled for a minute then realized who Heather meant. "Owen. Owen Scott. I didn't realize he was coming, too." She scanned the crowd to see if she could find the young man who was her assistant at the library, and also in charge of the building's conference services. She suspected she'd see his hair first: when he let his hair get more than an inch long, he suddenly became the modern-day version of the Heat Miser, only with brown instead of red hair.

Sure enough, using Owen's hair as a beacon, Megan quickly found him and waved at him. He waved back with a look of relief and jogged over.

"Owen, Heather. Heather, Owen," Megan said. "Heather is the Assistant Director. She's in charge of us." Megan and Lily exchanged glances without even looking at each other, as only best friends can.

"Nice to meet you," Owen said. He caught the invisible exchange between Megan and Lily, and suppressed a smile.

Heather pursed her lips.

"All of you to wardrobe, please," Heather said. "We don't really need you but Edison wants you here, so …" The gym site included a small paved parking lot in the front of the building, the river side, which fed into an unpaved area that started in the front and spilled into a very large area around the back that could also be used for parking or, in this case, as a temporary home for trailers for the cast and crew and general filming purposes. Heather pointed them in the direction of the unpaved area near the front. "First trailer over there. You can't miss it." She walked away, pursing her lips, and seemed to forget them almost immediately.

"She's really sweet," Megan commented.

"Quite friendly and welcoming," Owen agreed. He absent-mindedly ruffled his own hair, making it bigger than ever. Megan had to stop herself from reaching over to ruffle it, as well. Owen's hair was one of her favorite things.

The trio walked toward the area Heather had pointed at and easily found the one that said WARDROBE in a makeshift sign over its door. There was a backup of people in line to get in, so they stood aside to wait. From this perspective they could see around toward the back, humming with activity. People were milling around everywhere, most of them focused and busy, some of them looking like they weren't yet sure what they were supposed to be doing. By the looks of the latter group—in particular their well-defined arm muscles—Megan guessed those must be the cast and climbers.

"I didn't know you were going to be an extra, too," Lily said to Owen. "I'm glad you're here! Have you climbed before?"

"Parker and I have come to River Rock a few times," Owen said, nodding his head back at the climbing gym. "We saw Edison here and he invited us to come check out the filming and be extras if we wanted to. Parker couldn't make it, but here I am." Parker was Owen's boyfriend.

"We've met the two lead male actors," said Lily. "Bee and Fox. I guess it's a requirement to be named after an animal? Or a bug? Anyway, we've met them, and now Heather. We don't know much more yet. How about you?"

"I met the writer-slash-producer," Owen said, looking around the lot. Finally he spotted his target, a man somewhere in his late thirties, his head either naturally bald or shaved. He wore dark-rimmed glasses and was dressed like many of the climbers. "Roman Shropshire," Owen said. "Also a climber, but not at the level of some of these guys; at least, that's what he told me. Past his prime, he told me, but passionate about the sport." He looked around again. "And over there, I met that woman with the curly blonde hair, the purple and yellow shirt, that's Shay Garrick. She's the female lead. Also a climber."

"A lot of climbers," Megan noted.

"Yeah, a few dirtbaggers but mostly they climb in their free time and have real jobs the rest of the time. The cinematographer, for example, is both cinematographer and climber."

"Dirtbaggers?" Lily said, raising a perfectly groomed eyebrow.

"A climber who more or less lives in his or her car," Owen explained. "They just want to climb. Living in their cars or vans lets them stay mobile and go where the climbing is."

"Quite a life," Megan said.

"Unencumbered," Owen said, shrugging. "They get to do what they want, live the life they want. That's not such a bad thing."

"But no showers," Megan said.

Owen laughed. "I think they use showers at park restrooms. When they can, anyway. But yeah, if you can't live without showers, dirtbagging might not be the life for you."

"I actually could see Edison doing that," Megan said, noticing the wealthy man heading toward them with the writer by his side. "I feel like he might like the freedom. The adventure." She stopped and smiled as Edison came within hearing distance.

"Hey, you guys!" Edison said. "So glad you're here. I want to introduce you to someone!"

"Quickly, though," Megan said, eyeing the diminishing line at the wardrobe trailer. "We'll get in trouble with Heather if we don't check in with wardrobe soon." From across the lot she saw the dark haired woman staring at them, lips pursed.

"Ah, let me worry about that," Edison said with an amused glance at the Assistant Director. "Megan, Lily, Owen, this is Roman Shropshire. Writer and producer of *Inner Ascent*."

"Nice to meet you," Megan said with outstretched hand. "*Inner Ascent*? That's the movie?"

"The story of how climbing changed a man," Roman said as he shook Megan's hand. "He's troubled, can't find his way in life. He discovers rock climbing and bouldering, and then discovers himself. Goes on to be a champion." He lifted a shoulder. "Sort of my story, I guess, minus the champion part. Who amongst writers doesn't pen at least one thinly veiled autobiography?"

"Maybe you could still become a champion," Lily said encouragingly and with the sweet charm only Lily could muster: pure, without the least hint of sarcasm, like everything was possible and no dreams were too big. "Do you mostly write screenplays?" she asked, shaking Roman's hand.

"Sure, mostly," Roman said, distracted. He gazed up at the outside climbing walls with a look of admiration and awe. "Edison, this is a dream come true. This set. It's like you built it for me. For this film. Even the speed climbing wall," he said, indicating the taller of the two walls, the one with identical routes on each side, scaling up the fifty-foot height. "I never did speed climbing but I'm definitely going to try that out myself." He looked at Megan. "I should have been born twenty years later. Climbers these days are at their peaks just barely after puberty. I didn't discover climbing until I was thirty. Hardly knew it was a thing. But these days it's everywhere."

"Even out here in Emerson Falls, thanks to Edison," Megan said. The more everyone talked about the sport, the more she couldn't wait to try it out.

"You're welcome to come back anytime, even after the film is done," Edison said to Roman. "I built this as a vanity project—I wanted it for myself. But I want to share it with everyone. There's something about climbing that's ... well, it's spiritual. You know. It's indescribable."

Edison's phone buzzed in his pocket, and he pulled it out to look at the screen. "Sorry. Looks like it's for you, Roman. Asher, one of my staff, is texting to tell me there's a journalist and photographer here to talk to you. Want me to tell him to have them go away?"

"No, no," said Roman, though his face showed a measure of distaste. "I asked them to come. Indie films, we need all the press we can get. Let Asher know I'm on my way. Nice to meet you all, don't let Heather scare you. Help yourself to catering," he said, waving toward some tables in the distance, laid out with a variety of nourishments from the sweet to the savory. "And thanks for coming. I hope you'll enjoy working with us and will help spread the word about *Inner Ascent.*" He nodded, then trotted off toward the lobby of the gym.

"I hear you're hosting Piper and Fox at the library for the course of the filming," Edison said to Megan as they watched Roman walk off. "I owe you one. It sounds like that could have blown up in many directions if Fox'd had to stay in a haunted hotel. Seems he and Roman have butted heads a bit on this project. And then there's the fact that half the climbers have a crush on Piper."

"Weird," said Megan. "I always imagined climbers would be a really chill group."

"I think they are, in general," said Edison. "But you can't get rid of egos." He shrugged. "Anyway, I should head off to meet those reporters, too. Can't hurt to get in a word about River Rock. And also I need to check in with my staff. This film crew has been ... shall we say, not as attentive to rules as we'd like them to be. It's stressing out my staff and I want to keep it all contained as much as possible. If you see any trouble, let me know. Megan, I'll check in with you about Piper and Fox. Any expenses, keep track of them, I'll cover it." He raised his eyebrows to let her know he was serious, then followed after Roman.

Megan caught sight of Heather, who had been watching them with a glare. "We'd better get into wardrobe," she said. "Before we are fired!"

Several hours later, after the director had called a wrap for the day, Megan found Piper and Fox. The day had mostly been spent preparing for the next day's shoot, getting logistics figured out, coordinating everyone's wardrobes, and putting out small fires.

No filming had been accomplished, at least that Megan had seen, but still she'd enjoyed the new experience and watching the strong, skilled climbers climb the walls while they waited.

"It's an easy drive to my place," Megan told Piper and Fox as they stood by their cars in the gym's small front parking lot. She'd offered to give them a ride but Fox had a rental car and was going to drive them himself. "It's pretty straightforward. You really almost can't get lost; there aren't that many roads. Just follow the road that goes along the river as far as it goes to the west," she said, pointing. "Then turn into the library parking lot and follow the curve around to the parking in the back, on the river side, and I'll meet you there. Or you can just follow me. That would be easiest."

"I forgot something in my trailer," Fox said with a glance at Piper. "I'll just be a second and then we'll catch up."

"See you in a minute," Megan said, and she drove off toward the library.

Assuming they wouldn't be long, Megan simply waited for the couple from the back parking lot of the library, watching the river flow by. She loved the way the sun glistened off the surface, the light so pure and bright it was hard to believe it was nothing but a reflection. She closed her eyes and took in the scents of the river: the clean water, the damp earth, the faint whiff of grass freshly cut by the groundskeeper that morning. Before too long, Megan heard the sound of another vehicle. She turned and waved at the climbers as they parked.

As Fox and Piper stepped out of their car, Piper looked around with wonder, her eyes popping. "Gorgeous!" she said. "This is where you live?"

"This is where I live! Nicer than a haunted hotel, eh?" Megan said.

Fox seemed not to hear her. He pulled their bags out of the trunk, and Megan picked up a suitcase to help.

"This way," she said. They headed into the back lobby and rode the elevator up to Megan's floor. "I need to get the keys for your room ... rooms?"

"Room," said Piper, smiling. "We can share."

"Do I not get a say?" Fox joked. He winked at Megan. "We can share."

Megan popped into her own apartment and grabbed two keys to her favorite of the guest rooms, the one with the best view of the river. When she got back to the hallway, Fox and Piper had their heads together, whispering and frowning, but they broke apart abruptly when Megan appeared. She pretended not to have seen the intimate moment, and led the couple down the hallway, opened the door, then handed them the keys.

"Your castle," she said, and she let them walk in ahead of her.

"Ohhhh, nice!" said Piper, looking around the large suite.

Megan walked to the window. "You can see the river from here," she said. "And down there, by the river, there's a fire pit and some chairs, a great place to sit. Tonight's a full moon; perfect night for it." She pointed off to the left. "You can sort of see over there, that's a riverfront trail if you want to go for a walk. It basically runs parallel to the road we just drove on, just closer to the river. There's a park, then another park with the waterfalls, and then after that you're back at River Rock, where you're filming. After that, you're at Edison's house."

Piper was nodding, taking it all in. Fox headed for the bathroom.

"Do you know a good place to eat?" said Piper, her eyes focused on the empty space where Fox had been. "Want to join us?"

"Yes to both," said Megan. "Best place in town: Rae's Pub!"

Ten minutes later, Megan had escorted Piper and Fox into a corner table and was at the counter filling a pitcher with ice and water.

The pub owner, Rae Norris, walked up, looking irritated. "What, you're doing my job now? You don't trust me to bring you water?"

Megan turned so her back was to Piper and Fox, then whispered conspiratorially. "No. I wanted to tell you who I'm sitting with," she said.

Rae waited a moment, but Megan didn't continue. "All right," Rae said finally. "Tell me. Who are you sitting with? The Queen of England? Prince Harry?"

"Better," said Megan.

Rae shook her head. "Megan Montaigne, you know patience is not my strong point." She filled a pitcher with ice and water for another table.

"Max's ex-girlfriend," Megan said, wiggling her eyebrows. "I'm sitting with Max's ex-girlfriend."

At this, Rae's interest returned. Slowly, she raised one eyebrow, then the other. "Oh *really*?" Without turning her head, she shifted her eyes toward Megan's table.

"Really," said Megan, grabbing her pitcher and three glasses. "We'll take a bottle of your best wine. Put it on Edison's tab."

"I will keep the bottles coming," Rae said, intrigued but shaking her head as Megan walked away. "Will you look at what the wind blew in," she mumbled to herself as she watched as Megan settled into the table with her guests. Rae clucked her tongue and went back to work, whistling.

While she brought the water over to the table, Megan finally had a chance to get a good look at Piper and Fox. Piper had an aura of calm and confidence. Her hair was light brown, long, with sun bleached strands, and she'd tied it back in a bun that managed to look both messy and fashionable at the same time—a look that Megan knew would take herself hours to replicate. Piper's eyes were big and wide and a green-brown hazel blend; her cheekbones were high and her skin was radiant, the

healthy glow of a person who spent a good amount of time outside doing what she loved.

Fox, sitting next to Piper, was lean, maybe just under six feet
tall. His dirty-blond hair was shaggy and unkempt, and made
him look a little like a surfer; his eyes were deep and dark and
distant. Megan had caught sight of his bare abdomen earlier in
the day when he was climbing. To say he had a six-pack would
be understating his muscles. More like an eight-pack, Megan had
thought. With two mini four-packs on either side. Was that even
possible? She'd wondered, yet her eyes hadn't been deceiving
her. The man was fit and strong. When Megan had shaken their
hands earlier, she'd noticed both Fox's and Piper's palms were
rough and calloused, with a few scraggly pieces of tape wound
around various fingers on each hand. Whether the tape was for
the movie or just part of their everyday care, Megan didn't know.

Megan slid into the seat next to Piper and poured water for
each of them. "Rae will be over in a minute. I forgot to mention
there's not really a menu. You just get what she's serving. If that's
a problem—"

"Oh that's fun!" Piper said, her eyes slipping to Fox's for his
approval.

"Works for me," he said, shrugging.

"If you want something other than what she brings, it's not a
problem. It's just how she does things. Always has. She's bringing wine, too, but if you prefer beer—"

"Just water for me," Fox said.

"I'd love a glass of wine," Piper said, smiling.

"So how did the day go for you guys?" Megan asked. "It didn't
look like there was any filming?"

"Mostly blocking," Fox said. "Setting up shots and so on. A lot
of the filming will be on location outside, but at the gym we're
doing some indoor shots and a couple of scenes on the speed
wall, I think."

"I think that's right," Piper agreed. "My role doesn't have any scenes at the gym, but I'm here for moral support." She leaned into Fox's side and smiled up at him.

"Did you see Donut and Bee?" Fox said, looking down at Piper. "Out back at one point. They were going at it. Donut can't get over Bee getting the lead role."

"Donut," Megan said, remembering Edison had told them that was someone's nickname and trying to remember who. "Why does ... uh ... Donut think Bee shouldn't have the lead role?" Megan asked, still wracking her brain.

"Because he wanted it himself," Piper said. "And you can call him Brenden, if you'd rather. I don't think he really likes the name Donut, to be honest."

"Good," Megan said. "Not sure I can call someone a breakfast pastry. So is Brenden a good climber?" Megan asked. "Why did Bee get the role over him?"

"Brenden is a better climber than Bee, and also a better actor," said Fox.

"So ...? I don't get it," Megan said.

Piper shifted in her seat uncomfortably. "I mean, everyone has different taste, right? Who's to say who's attractive and who isn't?"

"Bee looks better on screen," Fox said, cutting to the point. "Donut is weird-looking."

"Ah," Megan said. Her heart dropped. She couldn't help but feel bad for Brenden. It wasn't fair for someone to get a role simply because they were more handsome. But that was Hollywood, she supposed. "I can see why he'd be upset. I would be, too."

"And also, Bee is an ass," Fox said. "An ass with an ego ten times the size of his head."

"Stop," Piper said. "Be nice."

"He keeps coming on to Piper, even though he knows she's

with me. Even though she's said no a million times." A muscle in Fox's neck twitched.

"I thought I saw him watching you," Megan said to Piper. "Something about his look made me uncomfortable."

"Yeah …" Piper said. "There's just something about him. I don't know what it is."

"He's an ass," Fox said.

Piper laughed. "Well, that's a broad way of putting it."

"Trust your instincts," Megan said. "I always say, trust your instincts. So, enough about him, though. How did you meet Max?" Her curiosity was killing her.

As if on cue, Rae came over with the promised bottle of her best wine, she set it out with three glasses. "Hello, I'm Rae, owner and proprietor and chef," she said. "Welcome. I hear we have a friend in common."

"Nice to meet you, Rae. I'm Piper," said Piper.

"Fox," said Fox. He waved his hand at the wine glass. "None for me."

"I was just asking how Piper met Max," Megan said.

"It was so cliché," Piper said, glancing again at Fox. "Through mutual friends, at a party. We clicked." She shrugged and said no more.

Megan noticed that Fox had stiffened up again, and realized this might not be the time to dive into everything she wanted to know.

Soon, Rae brought over their dinner: a cranberry spinach salad with chicken cordon bleu for the entree. Piper and Fox declared the meal to be fantastic. Piper and Megan drank the wine. Fox, Megan noticed, seemed to brood, even through his attempts to be congenial and friendly. Finally, the meal ended and Megan told them it was Edison's treat.

"Thank you, Edison," Fox said, though his tone suggested a bit of entitlement. He looked at his watch. "You said there's a trail along the river? I think I might want to go for a run in a half an hour or so. Full moon and whatnot."

"Beautiful night for it," Piper said. "I might go, too. It's safe, right?"

"I've seen a Canada lynx on that trail before," Megan said. "But I don't think they eat humans. It'll be dark, but it's unlikely anything will attack you. I doubt any bears would come down, but it's possible. Just keep your eyes open. Here, give me your phone and I'll enter my contact info." Piper handed Megan her phone and Megan tapped away. "If you need anything, just holler. Edison has given me full authority to take care of whatever you need."

"Amazing. Thank you," said Piper. She looked at Fox, then back to Megan. "You can head on home without us. I think we'll walk back to the library, if that's okay? That wine was delicious but I think it's gone to my head," she said. "I could use some fresh air."

"No problem," Megan said. She waved at Rae on her way out the door, and headed home where she set about some chores before eventually heading to bed for an exhausted, dreamless sleep.

The next morning, the blare of sirens rushing by startled Megan awake.

Police? Ambulance?

Both?

Megan looked at the clock. Six-thirty.

What day was it?

She thought hard, clawing through the web of sleep.

Sunday. The library was closed. She blinked to help herself remember. She was due at the film set at ten.

The sound of sirens near the library was unusual. First, sirens were unusual in general in Emerson Falls. Second, most locations in Emerson Falls would be reached without coming by the library.

Where could it be headed?

Suddenly, wide awake, Megan sat up.

Edison. Edison's house.

The library was at one end of the river road. At the other end, just past the climbing gym, was Edison.

Megan reached for her phone to see if anyone had texted her with any alerts or news. Rae was an early riser, and Rae always was the first to know. Surely if there was something important going on, Rae would have texted.

But there were no messages.

Megan wished for a police scanner. She knew it would be pointless to go online. The locals were far more inclined to stand at their front doors gossiping than they were to go post something online. And while the isolated location of the library was much to her liking, it also meant she didn't have any neighbors.

How to find out what was happening?

She didn't want to be an ambulance chaser. But she did want to go chase that ambulance. Or police car. Or whatever it was.

She texted Edison. *Are you okay? I heard sirens.*

She waited.

No reply.

Megan lolled in bed another half hour but couldn't sleep. She got up and showered. Dried her hair. Got dressed. Made herself a strong cup of coffee. Sat down on the balcony off her bedroom and watched the river and tried not to worry.

When she looked at her phone again, Edison had returned her text.

Accident at the gym. Enzo Larrabee. Bee. He's dead.

THREE

All activities related to filming are canceled today. Please await further instructions.

The text from Heather Birdsong, the dark and angular Assistant Director, came through moments after Edison's message.

Megan stared at the text as if it might have more answers.

An accident, Edison had said. An accident at the gym.

Megan put on her shoes, grabbed her purse, and headed to River Rock.

When she pulled her car into the parking lot, she saw she was not the only one with that idea. The gym itself, the tall speed climbing wall, and a good bit of space around both were cordoned off with bright yellow tape, rippling gently with the soft summer breeze. Small groups of people, many of whose faces Megan recognized from the day before, were huddled together. Arms wrapped around each other in comfort. Eyes red. Mouths agape with disbelief. Staring at the climbing wall and the ground beneath it or staring blankly into space. Shock.

Megan looked around until she saw Edison. He was with two

people who Megan thought were his staff. She didn't want to disturb them so she waited. After a few minutes, he nodded at the two people and they walked off into the gym, while Edison stood, looking lost. Megan made her way over to him.

"I'm so sorry, Edison," Megan said, putting a hand on his arm. "What happened?"

Edison shook his head. "Lexi, one of my staff, got here at six to open up the gym and get everything ready for the crew. As she was walking up to the front door, she saw a lump on the ground at the base of the speed climbing wall," he said, nodding his head toward the fifty-foot wall that was attached to the side of the gym. "She looked closer, and …" he took a deep breath. "It was Enzo." He shook his head again. "What a horrible thing to encounter. Lexi didn't touch him. He wasn't moving but she was too scared to touch him and see if he was breathing. She called 911. They came. He was dead."

"Do they know what happened, though?" Megan said. She looked up to the top of the speed climbing wall. It was very, very high, and though there was a cushion at the base, it would not necessarily protect a person from a bad fall. That's why there were ropes.

"We've been looking through the CCTV," Edison said. "There are two cameras out here, that are on all the time. Last night after the crew had gone home, Enzo showed up and just started climbing. But the weird thing is, he didn't clip in to the auto belay."

"The auto belay?" Megan said.

"The rope mechanism. When you are climbing with someone, that other person will belay you—that is, they hold the other end of the rope to catch you if you fall. But you can also clip into an auto-belay system, which means you can climb without a partner. On the speed climbing wall, you use an auto belay because you're climbing too fast for a person to belay you. Some people climb that whole wall in less than six seconds," Edison said, the last part almost as an aside.

Megan looked up to the top of the wall again. People could climb that in less than six seconds?

"So he wasn't using the rope?" Megan said. "That seems insane."

"Well, he wasn't climbing fast," Edison said, his brow furrowed. "It's weird. He started out just climbing the bottom section, slowly, like he was trying to cement it into his muscle memory. The thing about the speed climbing walls is that every wall is exactly the same. It's a competition route. People all around the world climb the exact same route, with the holds placed at the exact same angle, everything is calibrated so it's the same no matter where you go." Edison sighed again. "Anyway, he climbed the first fifteen feet or so several times, downclimbing each time—that is, rather than jumping off the wall or falling on the rope, you climb back down the way you came up. Then he climbed a little farther. And a little farther each time."

"How can a person do that, though? It looks impossible," Megan said.

"The thing about the speed climbing wall is it's not designed to be super difficult to climb. It's only a 5.11a, I think. That's a part of the grading system. For skilled climbers, it's not hard. The hard part, and the dangerous part, is doing it fast." He paused. "If you ask me, it was pure arrogance. Not to disparage the dead, but it was a stupid move. He wanted to practice it so he could climb it without a rope, fast."

"But why?" Megan said.

"Ego," Edison said. "And he did it. Eventually, he climbed all the way to the top, really without any problems. But then when he hit the last hold, suddenly he lost it and ..."

"The end," Megan said.

"The end," Edison repeated somberly.

"Megan!"

Megan and Edison turned toward a female voice headed their way. Piper was walking briskly across the gravel parking lot, her face crunched with concern. Her hair was again pulled back into a messy bun, her feet were in flip flops, and the clothes she was wearing might have been her pajamas. As if she, too, had rushed over the moment she heard.

Piper nodded at Edison. "What happened? I'm hearing so many rumors. It's really Bee?" She looked up at the speed climbing wall. "I heard …?"

Megan nodded. "It looks like an accident. Like maybe he was … I don't know, practicing, so he could impress someone."

Piper's eyes flashed wide. "You think he was doing this to impress me?"

"Oh, no," Megan said, quickly backtracking. "Not necessarily you. Someone. Anyone." She paused. "You did say he had quite an ego."

Piper looked at the top of the tall wall again. "Yeah. Yeah, he did." She shook her head. "They said he was here late last night. But what time? I was here last night, when I was out on a run. I didn't see anyone on the wall. There was a car …" she trailed off, trying to remember. "But no one on the wall."

"What time were you here?" Edison said.

"I don't know, late but not too late. Eleven? Or Midnight?"

Megan's eyebrow rose. Eleven or midnight was not "late but not too late" to her, but to each their own.

Edison nodded slowly. "He was dead by then," he said.

Piper gasped. The rising sun was already warming the air, but she hugged herself like she was chilled to the bones. "He was … so … he was on the ground?" The color had drained from her face. "And I didn't see him?"

"Wasn't Fox with you?" Megan said. "I thought you guys were going on a run together."

Piper closed her eyes slowly. "We had a fight. He went off on his run, I went off on mine."

"Sorry," Megan said. "Sorry to hear that."

Piper waved a hand dismissively. "It's no big deal."

Suddenly, a thought occurred to Megan. "Edison, you don't think they'll sue you, do you?" The gym was brand new. She would hate for it to close so soon due to a lawsuit.

Edison laughed sardonically. "My lawyers could eat their lawyers for breakfast. River Rock, my staff, me, everything associated with this gym are completely free from any liability. They signed it all away. Besides, everything was locked." He frowned. "How did he even get past the fence?" Tall iron fences surrounded each outside climbing wall. The walls were generally accessed from inside the gym for safety and control purposes, but they could be opened or retracted in sections for better viewing if there was a competition—or a film crew that needed space to film. But the fences were carefully closed and locked every night.

"Maybe he climbed over?" Piper said. "Climbers have been known to do that."

"Such a mess," Megan said. "And, not that this is the most important thing, but what will they do about the movie? About his part?"

Piper raised an eyebrow. "Word is Roman has asked Brenden to take on Bee's role. And Brenden has said yes. Filming will start up again tomorrow, or as soon as this is all cleared. The show must go on." She shrugged and then hugged herself again.

Edison pulled his buzzing phone out of his pocket. "The press are here," he said. "I guess I need to think of something to say." He craned his head to look up at the top of the wall that had been Bee's demise. "This is not the dream I had," he said. "This is not at all the dream." He walked away slowly, head down in thought.

"I'm going to find Roman," Piper said. "Text me if you hear anything."

Megan wasn't sure what Piper thought Megan might hear, but she nodded.

From beyond the police tape, Megan stared at the ground at the base of the wall. Bee's body was long gone and a few forensics investigators were still milling about, but it looked like their work was mostly done and they were packing up to leave. Just like that, a life over.

Megan turned to head back to her car. Nothing more she could do here, and if anyone needed her, they knew how to reach her. As she walked, she saw a piece of paper littering the parking lot. Looking around for a trash can, she leaned down to pick the paper up. One side was blank. She turned it over. A short note was written on it: "Speed wall tonight?"

Megan frowned. Probably it was nothing. Coincidence. Nonetheless, she put the note in her purse, inside a small zipper bag in which she kept her business cards.

From whom? To whom? Tonight as in last night?

The CCTV had shown all the activity of the evening. It was an accident.

Wasn't it?

FOUR

It was just past ten a.m. when Megan left the gym. She drove home on autopilot, hardly noticing the road, the river, the park, all her favorite places in her favorite town on the planet. "Speed wall tonight?" kept rolling around in her mind. Who had written the note? To whom? Was that why Bee was there? Was anyone else there, watching?

The gym hadn't been open long, but that didn't mean the note couldn't be old. It didn't look worn and weathered, but they'd had several weeks of picture-perfect weather, the kind that drew tourists in droves. Including out-of-towners wanting to test out the new rock climbing gym, Megan thought, with a twinge of pride on Edison's behalf.

But a note that said "speed wall tonight?" indicated two people, at least two, who for some reason were communicating with written notes rather than texts or calls. It meant a note passed from one person to another, maybe via a third party, maybe not. Could the note have been left for someone? At the front desk? On a car? In a bag? Had the sender and the recipient even talked about it?

Megan pulled her car around to the back parking lot at the library and parked. She reached into her purse for her phone.

Lunch at Rae's, 11:30.

She tapped out the message, hit "send," and the text flew into the ether to Lily, Owen, Max, and Rae. Then she headed up to her apartment. She needed coffee, and air, and to sit and stare at the river.

Soon Megan was out on her balcony, her favorite yellow mug filled with coffee and warming her hands. She settled into one of her Adirondack chairs and breathed a sigh of relief. A morning that started with sirens was unsettling.

Sipping the warm brew, Megan let her gaze fall on the river. The balcony of her apartment looked out over the Skagit River, and its ceaseless flow always offered Megan both calm and perspective. The gentle shushing of the water, the endless progress of the droplets of water from mountain to ocean, back up into the air, then down again as rain and snow to start over again, it reminded her of the eternal cycles of life, and how small she was, how small all humans were, how inevitable death was from the moment of birth.

Still, to die at Bee's age, whatever that might have been, was far too young.

What had driven him? What pushed his ego to the point of danger? What insecurities made him think that climbing faster than someone else, without safety ropes to keep him secure, would in any way matter?

"Maybe I'll ask Piper later," Megan said, out loud, to the river, and any eagles that might be flying by. "I definitely want to talk more to Piper."

She thought then about Piper. Piper and Max. Megan hadn't really had time to think about them yet, them together, as a couple, and as the thoughts crept into her mind she felt a resistance to them. Part of her didn't want to think about it. Piper was sweet, and smart, and strong.

Why had Max left?

Did Piper want him back?

And then, as with Bee's need to climb farther and faster, Megan had to as herself: what did it matter? She wasn't dating Max, and even if she was, Piper was in the past.

A funny thing, love, Megan thought. Jealousy. Attraction. Desire.

Revenge.

The thing that had been tickling at the back of Megan's brain burst to the front.

Fox. Fox and Bee. The look Bee had daggered in Fox's direction when Fox wrapped his arm around Piper. Bee's feelings of rejection. What was the story there? Had promises been made and broken? Could an ego that refused to believe it needed to clip into a safety device also refuse to hear the word "no"?

Or, speaking of rejection, Brenden. Wanting the acting role but not having the right look. And, interestingly enough, he might now have the role he wanted all along. Was that by chance? Or by his own design?

So far, everything pointed to an accident.

But she wondered.

That common phrase, "There are no accidents."

Megan sipped her coffee, and stared at the river, and thought.

The day was too beautiful, and Rae's wasn't far away, so Megan walked the short distance to the pub. When she got there shortly before eleven thirty, the rest of her crew were already seated at their favorite table in the corner.

"Hey," Megan said, slipping in next to Owen.

"Hey, boss," said Owen.

"Hey," said Lily, her voice a melody.

"Fancy meeting you here," Max said, his dimples beaming.

"Fancy, indeed!" The pub seemed especially dark after her short walk out in the sunshine, and with her heart heavy from the death that morning, Megan felt the lack of light more than usual. "Rae really needs to set up some outside seating," she said as the proprietor with the short white-blonde hair approached. "What do you say, Rae? Some seating outside, out back? Get those big heat towers for the cold nights? Set it up with bistro lighting?"

"Ooh, yes! And a little stage for some local musicians to serenade us?" Lily joined in, her eyes bright with the idea.

Rae sniffed and tossed a dish towel over her shoulder. "Funny you should mention that," she said.

"Are you doing it?" Megan said, clapping. "Are you really? Setting up some outside seating?"

"I merely said that it's funny you should mention that," Rae said, but a hint of amusement in her eyes broke through. "You'll just have to wait. Now. Lunch is burgers. They'll be out in a minute. Why have you called everyone here?"

Megan reached into her purse and pulled out the plastic bag with the note from the parking lot. She placed it on the table.

"This," she said.

"Oh, a plastic bag! With paper!" Owen said, but he was studying the bag carefully. He tilted his head to see better.

Max picked it up so he could read the writing. "Speed wall tonight?" he said, then looked at Megan. "What is this? Who wrote this?"

"That, dear Watson, is the question, isn't it? I found that in the parking lot at River Rock," Megan said.

"When?" Max asked. "Today?"

"Today," Megan said. "This morning as I was leaving."

"And you put it in a plastic bag? Look at you, Nancy Drew," said Owen, smiling.

"You're a poet, and you don't know it," Megan mocked back. She sighed. "So, I know everyone has said Bee's death was an accident, but … I just can't help but feel there's something off about it."

"Megan, they looked through all the film," said Lily gently. "Nothing is off. It was an accident."

Max nodded slowly.

Megan noticed. "You agree with me, don't you, Max? I see it. I know you. Why are you nodding?" she said.

Max shrugged. "No, go on. Why do you think something is off?"

"Instincts," Megan said.

"Instincts backed up by what?" Max said, nodding again.

Megan leaned in. "Okay. Yes. Backed up by a lot of things. Bee wasn't popular. Fox didn't like him because Bee kept hitting on Piper. For that matter, Piper may not have liked him." Megan thought Max's shoulders stiffened ever so slightly at the mention of Piper, but he kept listening. "And Brenden—some of them apparently call him Donut—the one who wanted Bee's role. He was bitter. And as luck would have it, with Bee gone, now Brenden is being asked to take on Bee's role." She raised her eyebrows to show how significant this was. "Hmm? See what I'm saying?"

"Someone is named Donut?" Max said, leaning back.

"You didn't hear?" Megan said. Without waiting for an answer, she continued. "Piper was out on a run last night, and she didn't see Bee, but she said there was a car at River Rock. Why was there a car there?"

"Did she say whose?" Max asked.

"She didn't," Megan admitted.

"Could it have been, like, maintenance? Custodial?" Owen asked.

Megan frowned.

Max leaned in again. "Well, Megan. It's funny you should mention that." He looked her in the eyes, studying her.

Megan waited for him to say more. "Go on?" she said after a moment.

"Edison gave me a call just before I got here," Max said.

"And?" Lily said. "Don't keep us hanging!"

"And you might be right," Max said. "His staff were on the speed wall after the police left, getting everything checked over and ready for filming again. They check the wall every morning, he told me. When they were checking the routes—both routes up both sides of the speed wall—they discovered something." Max nodded.

"Oh, Max. Stop with the dramatic timing," Owen said. "Blurt it out."

"At the top of the speed wall," Max said, drawing the wall with his hands, "the top holds have more than one screw securing them to the wall. There's the main screw, but then there's also what they call the set screw. It's extra insurance to make sure the hold stays where it's meant to, and doesn't spin when you grab onto it."

"If a hold were to spin," Megan said slowly, imagining the scenario, "it would … well, it would throw a person off the wall, wouldn't it? They'd fall?"

"Exactly right," Max said, nodding.

"And the set screws on Edison's speed wall routes…?" Megan said, anticipating the answer.

"The set screws on the top holds on both routes had been completely removed," Max said. "Something that had to be a deliberate act. Something that takes a special drill. Something a person would have to know how to do."

The table fell into silence as everyone absorbed the situation.

"Half the cast and crew are climbers," Megan said finally. "More than half."

"But they looked at the film," Lily protested. "They didn't see anyone messing with the routes. Did they? I thought it just showed Bee, climbing up and down the wall over and over. Nothing more."

"They hadn't looked back far enough," Max said. "Turns out for a period of time after the shooting was over for the day, but before Bee showed up, the cameras were somehow turned off."

"So it had to be staff?" Megan said, feeling a lump in her stomach. She'd hate for that to be the case. Poor Edison.

"The film crew had several keys," Max said.

"But how …?" Megan said. "Who?"

"That's what we have to find out," Max said.

"If the footage is gone, though …" Owen said tentatively.

"We start looking for motives," Max said. He turned to Megan. He cleared his throat. "Why don't you start by talking to Piper. I think she might be more open with you than with me." His thoughts turned inward for a moment but then he was his professional self again. "You and I will touch base then and I'll follow up on what you learn. Oh, and when you do, don't tell her any of what we've just learned from Edison. Let her do the talking. Anything she tells you, it's all new to you."

Megan nodded. "On it. But doesn't it have to be someone with access to the holds at the top of the wall? Someone who knows about the special drill?"

"I'm guessing a lot of people on that cast and crew know about set screws. Climbing is part of their lives. They'd know. At this point, we're just looking for leads. It could be two people working together who you'd never think were together. Motives can be funny things. Don't rule anything out yet. Be open."

"Yes, sir," Megan said.

"Owen and Lily," Max continued, "you have ears in the community. Today the filming is shut down, so people will be out and about and for sure there will be gossip. If you hear something, and there's a way to engage yourself in the conversation, try to find out more. Were there troubles on set? Not even just between Bee and someone, but between anyone. You never know where a trail will lead. And of course, if something catches your ear, let me know immediately."

"Will do," Lily said.

"No problem," Owen said.

Max tilted his head toward the restaurant's patrons. "Rae, I don't have to tell you to keep an eye out. You always know things before even I do!" He laughed. "But it looks like there are some crew and cast here today, and likely more will come in. Today and through the time they're here filming. Keep an extra ear open for anything that could be a clue."

"How much are you paying?" Rae said with a tiny smile.

"Same as always," Max said, dimples dimpling. "All of my love, to the end of time."

Rae swatted Max affectionately on the back. "You scoundrel," she said, but she walked away humming happily to go serve other customers.

Sunshine from outside streamed in as the front door opened. The group of people who entered, however, were somber, their voices subdued.

"Fox and Piper," Megan noted quietly, seeing the climbers among the newcomers. "And Roman, the writer-slash-producer." She chewed on her lip a moment. Would now be a good time to separate Piper from the group for a conversation? If only Rae's outside seating area were complete—Megan now assumed an outside seating area was a sure thing, eventually—Megan could sweep Piper away for a private conversation. But maybe …

Megan stood, looked at Max and wiggled her eyebrows once, meaningfully, then headed over to Piper. Fox had gone to the bar to get drinks.

"Hey," Megan said to Piper.

Piper looked up, startled, then relaxed. "Oh, hey."

"How are you doing?" Megan asked.

"Honestly, not so great. It's just awful," Piper said. Her eyes were slightly puffy, lined with red.

Megan nodded in solidarity. She looked around the room. "It's so noisy in here. Do you want to go back to the library with me? I've got wine. There's that fire pit I showed you, by the river. I always am so comforted by the river. We can talk it all through." Megan stopped, realizing she was about to start sounding desperate. She paused, letting silence speak.

Piper looked to where Fox was standing at the bar, talking to another person from the set. "I think Fox wants to stay here," she said.

"Fox can stay here," Megan said, and again she left the rest of her statement unspoken. If Piper and Fox had recently had a fight, Piper might be more open to the idea.

Piper's eyes stayed on Fox, but she nodded. "Yeah." She paused a few moments, then stood up. "Hang on, I'll tell him."

Piper walked over to the bar, exchanged a few words with Fox. He looked up and over at Megan, then, for some reason, at Max. Megan tried to read his expression. Annoyed? Happy? Noncommittal, was more like it. He didn't seem to care. Piper gave him a kiss on the cheek—which he also didn't seem to care about—then returned to Megan.

"Okay?" said Megan.

"All good," Piper said.

Megan did not think all was actually good, but she left it alone. "I walked here," Megan said. "Do you mind walking?"

"Nope," Piper said, though her mind still seemed to be back

with Fox.

As they exited the front door, Piper's attention was drawn to a car in the parking lot. "Oh," she said. "That's Roman's car."

"Roman's car?" Megan asked as they started walking toward the library.

Piper pointed at a steel blue sedan. "That's the car I saw last night at the gym, when I was out on my run."

"Oh?" Megan said. "Did he confirm it? Did he say why he was there?"

"He said he forgot his phone charger," Piper said. "He didn't notice Bee, either. He was down in the trailers, which are around the other side. He didn't pay attention to the speed wall, he said. But I do wonder, if he'd seen Bee, could Bee have been alive? Could he have been saved?" She took a breath. "Or if I had seen him?" She shuddered.

Megan pondered a moment. She didn't want to let on anything about the loosened holds, but she did want to get more information.

From the treetops came a sound that was a cross between a dog's squeaky toy and a child's laugh. Megan looked up toward the trees and smiled. "Cooper's hawk," she said. "Might be a male telling the female where he is."

"Nice of him," Piper laughed. "Good communication skills."

The time seemed right. Megan jumped in. "Speaking of good communication skills," she said. "Max. He's got pretty good communication skills."

Piper seemed startled at the transition in conversation, but her face brightened in a nostalgic, sad sort of way, like good memories long gone. "Yeah. Probably better now than before, but ... not bad," she said.

"Were you together long?" Megan asked. She pointed to the left, indicating that they should turn down the road that would lead them past Lily's B&B and to the library. The sky was clear and blue, a perfect summer day. It was hard to believe it had started with the shock of a death. It made Megan think that every day was like this: perfect somewhere for someone, horrible elsewhere for someone else. She wondered who had called Bee's family to tell them the news. Had it been Max? She didn't envy him that part of the job.

"Two and a half years," Piper said. "It was good. Max is a good guy."

"He definitely is," Megan said.

Piper caught something in Megan's voice and looked at her. "What about *you* and Max?" Piper said inquisitively, with a light smile.

"Oh, no," Megan said, feeling awkward. "I mean, we've gone to dinner a couple of times. But we're friends."

Piper was silent for a bit. "Well, don't let him get away, if you get him," she said, finally.

"What do you mean?" Megan said. A large rock had fallen into the road on her path, so she kicked it gently off to the side of the road again. A black and orange butterfly flew by lazily on its haphazard path.

"He broke up with me," Piper said, "but later he told me he did so because I was already gone. 'I left because you pulled away first,' he told me. 'I just finished the job.' That stung. But he was right. I couldn't stay in it with him." Piper took a breath and looked up at the trees again, maybe for the cooper's hawk that was telling its mate he was near. "Have you heard of the idea that people can only love others as much as they love themselves? I think there's another side to it. I think people can only accept as much love as they can accept from themselves. Max wanted to love me so much. I didn't love myself. So I pushed him away. He wanted to give me more than I could accept." She was quiet again for a while. "Maybe that's why I'm with Fox now. He isn't able to give that much love."

"Ouch," Megan said. She wasn't sure what else to say.

"Yeah," Piper said. "But I'm working on it. Working on the loving myself part. We'll see where Fox fits in."

"So Fox isn't the jealous type at least, I guess?" Megan said, trying to work the conversation around to motives.

Piper's sudden laugh, a barking chirp that could have been a response cry to the hawk, gave Megan her answer. "No. Fox isn't jealous. Not about me, anyway. About other climbers, maybe, but not about me."

"About other climbers?" Megan asked.

"Most of the climbers are pretty laid back—at least, the climbers I know," Piper said. "I mean that's it, right, it's about the competition with yourself. It's you against gravity, not you against someone else. That's what I love about it. It's like life. You're sure to fall. If you're in it at all, you're sure to fall. You just have to keep getting yourself back up. Climbing is a great metaphor for life. And most of the climbers get that. But some of them, it's all about the competition. Their egos tell them that being better than others matters. That where they are in relation to someone else matters. I mean look at Bee. He thought that. His ego killed him."

"Who do you think he was trying to impress?" Megan asked. "Who would inspire that kind of … I mean, that's crazy, right, to do that wall without a rope?"

Piper sighed heavily. "You know, climbing the last few years, it's gotten a lot of press. The speed wall isn't technically that difficult. It's 5.11a."

"Edison mentioned that," Megan said.

"Yeah. It's just when you add the speed to it that it makes it harder. The weird thing is if you were practicing for speed, you wouldn't practice without the rope. Practicing the wall without a rope is just … I mean it's just climbing. To practice for speed you need to practice with speed, if that makes sense. I think he was just … well, either he wanted to impress someone or he just wanted to get better. Why he didn't clip into the belay, I don't know. It's just a crazy accident. Maybe it was just his time." She heaved a great sigh and looked up at the clouds.

The library was just ahead of them now, and as always, Megan's heart filled with gratitude for this beautiful building on this beautiful river. Edison and his ex-wife had built this four-teen-thousand-square-foot building as a vacation home. When Edison divorced her, he donated it, gleefully, to be renovated into a library. Now it was Megan's mission to make it into a cen-terpiece of the community, and she was already having great success. What's more, she got to live on the top floor.

"Shall I go up and get some wine? Meet you at the fire pit?" Megan said.

"You know, I'm actually tired," Piper said. "I think I may take a nap."

"No problem," Megan said, and they went upstairs togeth-er. Megan turned into her apartment, and Piper went into the guest sweet.

A few minutes later, Megan was out on her balcony with a cup of coffee, looking out over the water. She was disappointed in herself. She hadn't gotten much out of Piper. But certainly Piper didn't seem to think Fox would have killed Bee on her behalf. So, then, who?

Her phone buzzed on the table with an incoming text. Edison.

Auto belay rope was cut, too. If Bee had clipped in, the rope wouldn't have saved him.

Megan put her phone down. Bee's death still could have been an accident, but it was looking more and more certain someone had wanted to make it happen intentionally.

Out of the corner of her eye, Megan saw movement, a flash of color. She turned and saw Piper walking briskly along the river path, talking on her phone.

"Short nap," Megan said to herself. Where was Piper going? And who was she talking to?

"Do you know," Megan said to a cooper's hawk she saw flying by, "I think I suddenly feel like going bouldering."

FIVE

When Megan got to River Rock, she realized what must have brought Piper back so quickly: based on the accumulation of TV vans, cameras, and reporters, it seemed a press conference had been called. Roman, the film's writer/producer, was standing in the center of a small forest of microphones and reporters holding various recording devices and phones in his face. His bald head seemed slightly sweaty and was reflecting the sunlight; Megan worried on his behalf whether he needed some sunscreen. He was still talking over his shoulder to someone behind him—Megan thought it might be Heather, the Assistant Director—but it looked like he was about to speak. Megan jogged over so she wouldn't miss anything.

Moments after she was within hearing distance, Roman turned to the cameras and his audience. He pushed his dark glasses up on his nose and cleared his throat.

"I am ... I'm beyond devastated ... to have to tell you today that Enzo Larrabee, known to his colleagues in the climbing community and among our own little filming family as Bee, fell to his death this morning in a tragic climbing accident," Roman said. He cleared his throat again, and shook his head a few times as if in disbelief of the news he had to deliver, as if trying to shake off the tragedy itself like a dog might shake off water.

"Bee was twenty-five years old, he was smart, he was funny he was a good friend to all," Roman continued. "A fantastic climber, a rising talent in the field of acting. His discipline, his perseverance, his desire to always improve himself drove his life. Unfortunately, these things also drove his death. Last night, after filming ended, he returned here to River Rock to climb this speed climbing wall. We don't know why. We don't know what made him think it was important. Maybe just a longing to get better, to be the best he could be. We don't know. We will never know."

Roman hung his head for several long moments, then looked up at the cameras again. "We have contacted his family and they are, as we are, distraught. They ask for privacy at this time. But …" Roman shook his head again. "But the show must go on. Another climber, Brenden Kogut will be filling the role as we continue filming. Our funders and our cast and crew are depending on us to go forward with this project, and we will not disappoint them. This film will be made now in honor of Bee." Roman held up a fist, as if he were raising a glass. "To Bee," he said.

The crowd of reporters, not expecting to be a part of the story, remained silent.

Roman looked around and sighed. "Any questions?"

A tap on Megan's shoulder made her turn around. Edison stood behind her, looking somber and tired.

"Hey," he said quietly.

"Hey," Megan. "How are you holding up?"

Edison tipped his chin up toward Roman. "He thought we should do this press conference," he said. "Seemed a bit uncalled for to me, if I'm honest. Seemed like we could have just put out a statement." He blinked hard. "All publicity is good publicity, Roman told me." Edison sighed heavily. "I'm not sure I believe that. Forever this will be known as the climbing gym where Enzo Larrabee died."

Megan put a hand on Edison's arm. "No," she said. "I mean, yes, for a while. But you'll make it more than that. And we, all your friends, we'll help. We'll figure this out. We've got this. Emerson Falls Strong."

Edison put a hand on top of Megan's "Thanks," he said sadly.

"Tell me more about the rope," Megan said. "I'm assuming your staff turned it over to Max?"

"Yeah," Edison said. "At first glance, they say it was a real painstaking job. Only because my staff are excellent did they even notice. It's like someone stuck the tip of a knife inside the rope and then cut the inside, while leaving the outside mostly intact. I don't know how long it would have taken for it to break, but a fall from the top of the wall almost certainly would have done it."

"Both ropes?" Megan said. "Both walls?"

"No, just the one side. The side Bee was on."

"The other rope was okay?"

"Seems to be, but like I said it was an almost invisible cut. We could have missed it. We're replacing both just to be sure. And they'll be going over every screw and every bolt on those holds today."

"Edison," Megan said, "Who would have had access?" She looked at the speed climbing wall, building a picture in her mind of what might have happened. "Where on the rope was it cut? How far from the ground? Meaning, would a person have to have been on the wall or a ladder to do it?"

Edison shook his head. "Not too far up. They could have pulled the rope out just a bit and done it that way. When a climber is clipped into the auto belay, the rope retracts as he or she climbs. If the cut had been high up, it could easily have gone through the pulley before anyone fell. That part of the rope would have been basically inactive and any climber would have been safe. By having the cut so close to where the climber clips in, it ensured that a fall would put stress on that point on the rope, and the rope would, or could, break."

"So the rope could have been cut from the ground," Megan said, still studying the wall.

"Easily," Edison said. "Most likely, really."

"But what about that top hold?" Megan said. "The one where the … the set screw was removed? How would a person access that? They'd need a ladder, wouldn't they?" A very tall ladder, she thought. The top of the wall was nearly five stories high. Where would a person even get a ladder that tall?

Edison wrapped his lips around his teeth for a moment. "Well, no," he said finally. "That wall is attached to the gym, right?" He pointed. The back of the speed climbing wall was flush with the side of the main building. "See how the whole thing is about four feet thick? Inside that, there's a series of ladders that go up to the top." He pointed to the top of the wall, fifty feet up. "I don't know if you can see it, but there's a panel up there, at the very top, that can be opened from the inside. The idea being that we can go up from the inside and perform maintenance on the pulleys at the top, if we need to, easily. And there are a couple other panels along the course of the wall to provide additional access. Without having to get out a crane. The top holds can be reached that way."

"So someone could climb up the inside of the back wall, poke their heads out of the top, and take out the set screw," Megan said.

"It looks like that might be what happened," Edison said. He squinted up into the bright sky, shielding his eyes, as he looked at the top of the towering wall.

"It would have to be someone who knew there was a ladder inside that wall," Megan said.

"It's not a huge secret," Edison said. "I'd say most of the cast and crew knew. A few of them asked about it, just casually, or at least I thought it was casual. And then people talk. People knew how it was built."

"Who asked?" Megan said. "Do you remember?"

"I guess the people who needed to know," Edison said. "Roman, the Set Director, the Assistant Director, plus a few of the actors who are climbers were just curious. Bee asked, I think. Fox was there when Bee asked. Shay Garrick, the female lead, she asked."

"Would they all know about the set screw?" Megan said. "The fact that it's there, and that it takes a special drill?"

"Could be," Edison said. "Easily could be. Most of them are climbers themselves. They know how it all works."

"But at least we rule out non-climbers," Megan said.

"Well, not necessarily," Edison said. "Someone else could have overheard."

"Which leaves us back at square one," Megan said. She clucked her teeth in frustration.

While they'd been speaking, the majority of the reporters had packed up and left. One woman, however, had stayed behind and was engaged in what seemed from a distance to be a somewhat hostile conversation with Roman.

"She doesn't look impressed," Megan said, drawing Edison's attention to the reporter in question with a nod of her head. "Wonder what that's about."

"That's the reporter who was here yesterday," Edison said. "I think she knows Roman somehow. He asked her to cover the filming, as a favor. I did a brief interview with her, too. Georgia …" Edison stopped and traced through his mind, trying to come up with a last name. "Torkelson. Georgia Torkelson. With the *Sedro-Woolley Gatherer*, I think, although I believe she also sells articles to bigger papers. At least, that's what she said."

The woman looked to be in her early thirties, with wavy ash-brown hair. She was dressed for the warm weather in a mustard-yellow knee-length sundress, and she wore a floppy white hat to protect her head from the sun. With her was a man in his forties, wearing wire-rimmed glasses, dressed in slacks, a short-sleeved white shirt, and a tie, who looked very much like he did not want to be there. The camera strapped around his neck strongly suggested he might be a photographer. This was confirmed when, to get away from the bickering pair, he started taking pictures of the speed climbing wall, the shorter climbing wall, the gym, the parking lot, the crowd of onlookers still lingering, and anything else he could focus his camera on. "I suppose someone in the entertainment industry might want the story," Megan said. "And now that there's been a death, the vultures will swoop in."

Roman and Georgia's exchange continued, both of their faces intense, their hands and arms waving and gesticulating to emphasize their points. Finally Roman put a hand up, signaling "Stop," and he turned and walked away, toward Megan and Edison.

"That woman," Roman said, shaking his head. "Edison, might I have a word?"

"Sure," Edison said. "Do you need someone to help … I don't know, get her off the premises or anything?"

"If you could get her out of my life, that would be better," Roman said, looking back at the woman with malice. "She's my ex-wife. Clinging to me like a barnacle on a sunken ship. A parasite, sucking the life out of me. A suckerfish, stuck to me for all eternity."

"I thought suckerfish were mutually beneficial, though?" Megan said, amusing herself. The look on Roman's face indicated he didn't share her amusement.

"A moment, Edison?" Roman said, tilting his head toward the gym, walking away.

The reporter, Georgia, had been watching Roman the whole time. Once he'd left, she made her way over to Megan.

"Georgia Torkelson," Georgia said. "Reporter with the *Sedro-Woolley Gatherer*." Still distracted by her ex-husband, she didn't hold out her hand.

"Megan Montaigne," Megan said. "Library Director for the Emerson Falls library, and extra in your ex-husband's movie."

At the words "ex-husband," Georgia's head snapped back to Megan. "He told you?"

"He did," Megan said. "But that's about it."

"Did he tell you he was supposed to pick up the kids to go to the park last night but he never showed?" Georgia said. "He told me he was coming to the Valley to do this movie and that would mean he'd have more time for the boys. But of course he hasn't followed through. And why would he? Why would he start now?"

"Is that what the … uh … conversation you were having was about?" Megan said. Georgia frowned. "Sorry," Megan said. "It was hard to miss."

"That, and everything else," Georgia said. "Hard to believe how much you can fit into one argument."

"Sorry," Megan said, though she wasn't sure exactly what she was sorry about. The whole situation, she supposed. The plight of humanity and interpersonal relationships. From which no one could escape.

Georgia sighed heavily, a sigh containing all the disappointment of a failed marriage. "I should have known," she said. "And I get to tell the kids again."

"It's nice of you to cover the story, though," Megan said. "Help him get publicity."

Georgia took off her floppy hat and ran a hand through her hair, which was slightly damp where the hat had been. The day was getting quite warm. "Well, it would be nice if he made some money for once. This is his first screenplay. Maybe this will be different. None of his books ever made much money and it would be nice for the kids if their dad could help them with their education one day. Although with the price of college these days …" She sighed again.

"Oh, he wrote books?" Megan said, her librarian ears perking up. "Anything I'd have heard of?"

"Almost certainly not," Georgia said with disdain. "He printed through a vanity press, appropriately enough. They charged him more than he ever made back on most of the books and barely lifted a finger to help with distribution. I kept telling him he should get the titles back and publish them himself. Instead, he started dating young female climbers behind my back and then asked for a divorce. A relief, really," she said. She checked the watch on her left hand, a dainty three-strand rhinestone bracelet attached to a small watch face. "I need to get this written up. Maybe a climbing magazine will take it," she said, mostly to herself. "If not one of the Hollywood rags." Georgia turned toward the photographer. "Bill!" she yelled, waving at him and then pointing toward the road. Time to go.

"Good luck," said Megan as Georgia quickly walked away.

Megan looked at the gym. Well, she thought, still time for a climb. Might as well.

The gym doors were wide open to welcome the fresh summer air. Megan walked up to the counter, where a young woman, her straw-blonde hair held back in a high ponytail, was seated.

"Hi," the woman said.

"Hi," Megan said. "I'm … uh … I'm an extra in the movie," Megan waved her hands toward the outside, where the filming hadn't yet happened. "I was wondering if I could climb today?"

"Are you a member?" the woman said.

"No, not yet, but I should be," Megan said. "Can I do a day pass or something? And I need shoes. Can I rent shoes?"

"No problem," the woman said. "I remember you now. You're Megan. I'm Lexi. I'm sure Edison would tell me to just let you go on in. Shoes are around the corner. Unisex. European sizes. There's a chart on the wall if you don't know yours. You want them tighter than your normal shoes. Let me know if you need help."

"Thanks," Megan said.

She quickly found the shoes and pulled out a pair, guessing at the sizes. As she was pulling them on—a bit of a struggle as they were so tight—another woman with a halo of curly blonde hair sat down next to her. She had a small bag and her own shoes, and based on the muscles in her arms, looked like she'd been climbing a while.

"Are these supposed to be this tight?" Megan asked the woman. Each shoe had two loops on the back, one on each side. Megan put her fingers through the loops and tugged.

The woman laughed. "Yeah, they are," she said. "In fact, if you're serious about it, they should be so tight that you don't even want to walk in them because they hurt."

Megan grunted as her foot finally slipped into the first shoe, and she started her effort with the other. "You're kidding," Megan said. "Why?"

"With climbing shoes you want to have as much contact as possible with the wall. You don't want a whole bunch of shoe between you and the rock. Imagine being on these walls in thick, insulated running shoes, almost an inch between the end of your toe and the tip of the shoe," the woman said, demonstrating with her hands. "On those tiny holds that are just half an inch deep. If you're in a shoe that has an inch of cushioning, your foot wouldn't even technically be touching the hold. Recipe for disaster." The woman smiled and held out a rough hand. "Shay," she said. "Shay Garrick."

"Oh, right," Megan said. "The actor."

Shay laughed. "I guess that's right. I think of myself as a climber first. But here we are."

"I'm so sorry about Bee," Megan said. "Did you know him well?"

Shay sobered. "Yeah, not close. Not really. I mean peripherally, everyone knows everyone." She paused. "He did ask me out when we first met, but like I said, we didn't really hang out."

"How long have you guys been filming?" Megan asked. "I mean before here. I know you're filming elsewhere, too."

"Over in Index, yeah," Shay said. "A few days there. I guess they'll have to reshoot some scenes with Donut now." Her eyes slipped away into thought. "Huh."

"Was Bee popular?" Megan asked. "Did people like him?"

Shay's thoughts snapped back to the present. "I mean, he was fine. He … well, I mean, just from his stunt, you know he was … he maybe had some misplaced priorities."

"What do you mean? His stunt?" Megan asked.

"His stunt," Shay said, nodding to the outside where the speed climbing wall was. "I get it, climbing the first dozen feet without a rope. But only a moron would climb the whole thing without a rope. You clip in. Even if you don't need the rope, you clip in. I don't know what he was trying to prove." She shook her head. "That's not true. I imagine he was trying to prove he was invincible. This whole movie thing was already going to his head. He imagined himself the star of the next big climbing documentary. *Free Bee* or something. But he didn't get it. He didn't realize it's not about taking big risks and it's not about fame. It's about becoming so good that what you're doing has very little risk for you. You maximize skill, minimize risk. Push the boundaries of your comfort zone by getting so good it's hardly even scary."

"Maybe that's what he was trying to do?" Megan said. "Become really good?"

"I suppose so," Shay said. She didn't seem convinced. "Still he should have clipped in. No reason not to. Some climbers … some of them just want to push the envelope, turn up the volume, push it all as far as it will go. They think they're immortal and they think living dangerously is what it takes to feel alive. You'll hear it every now and then, 'I'd rather live thirty years fully alive than eight years half dead.' I mean, I get it. But also I don't think they've really thought it through. The really good climbers, the ones who get to the highest levels, generally aren't quite as reckless. In my opinion, anyway."

"Where did Bee fall on that spectrum?" Megan asked. "Was he reckless?"

Shay shrugged. "Yeah, I guess he was. His death pretty much proves that, right? I think he may have bought into the whole image of himself as the golden boy. The chosen one. He may have believed it a bit too much."

Megan pushed. "It sounds like maybe he wasn't your favorite person. Did anyone really not like him? Were people jealous, or did they think he was crowding the spotlight too much?"

Shay's eyes slid to Megan's. "Why?" she asked.

"Just curious," Megan said.

Shay pulled her shoes out of her bag and started pulling them on, a question forming on her face. "Is it true, than?" she said. "They're saying it might not have been an accident."

"I don't know that," Megan lied. "But if it weren't an accident, who do you think would have wanted to hurt him?"

Shay thought a moment, then shook her head. But Megan could tell there was an answer rattling around inside Shay's mind.

"No, really," Megan said. "Who are you thinking?"

"I mean I don't want to cast aspersions on anyone or anything. What do I know?" Shay said.

"I'm not going to put handcuffs on the person you name," Megan said. "Or people. I'm just curious."

Shay finished tying her shoes and pulled the top part of her hair up into a ponytail. "Brenden is pretty excited to be in a lead role now, is what some people are saying. But what I think is that Fox is a lot happier without Bee." She stood and pushed her gym bag and street shoes into a small empty cubby in a wall of cubbies next to the shoes. "Later," she said, and she headed off to the bouldering section of the gym. As she did, she walked by Roman, who was heading back toward the lobby. Edison was nowhere to be seen. As Shay passed Roman the writer reached out and put his hands on Shay's shoulders, caressing them with an intimate familiarity. From the look on Shay's face, Megan could tell the touch wasn't welcome. Shay expertly shrugged Roman's hands off her, and quickly she scaled a route of black holds up to the top of the wall.

Roman's eyes followed Shay, lingering on her body, leering at her taut muscles. He smiled an amused smile and chuckled to himself. He then saw Megan watching him, and his face lost all expression. He looked away. The smile returned and he walked out of the building.

SIX

Megan jogged in place for two seconds before she decided her shoes were too tight for that. "These are not jogging shoes," she told the wall of shoes.

She then stood looking at the vast gym, unsure where to begin. The day before, she and Lily, Max, and Owen, the "extras Edison had insisted on" as Heather had put it, hadn't technically been needed. Edison had invited them to come early, so once they'd met with wardrobe to get everything squared away, they mostly sat around outside trying to stay out of the way and watch the ongoing activities. Megan had been mesmerized by the behind-the-scenes workings, and they'd all been fascinated to watch the climbers climb the outside walls when they weren't needed.

However, all of that meant that Megan hadn't yet stepped inside the gym. She felt like a bad friend. Even if technically she and Edison weren't good friends, she liked him a lot and was looking forward to spending time with him outside of Library Board meetings. He had blossomed since his divorce, like a man reborn. Seeing his passion for this new gym had been heart-warming. To see his dream crushed by tragedy was devastating.

She looked around, getting her bearings. The lobby was at the center point of a wide, upside-down, lopsided V that opened out toward the parking lot in front, the road before it and the river beyond. The shorter end of the V was at the east end, and at its end was the shorter climbing wall, the one built to look like an actual rock face. The speed climbing wall was on the end of the longer side of the V, on the west. The offices, staff areas, and storage were behind the lobby and extending to the left. The shoes and storage cubbies were by the lobby, along with the restrooms.

As Megan stood, uncertain about what she was supposed to do, she sensed a movement behind her. She turned to see Brenden putting on his shoes. As he laced up his tight climbing shoes, his eyes were glazed over, his thoughts distant.

"Hey," Megan said softly.

Brenden looked up, eyes focusing. "Hi," he said.

"So sorry about Bee," Megan said.

Brenden gave his laces a hard tug and finished tying his shoes. "Crazy," he said.

Megan turned back to assess the gym. On the left, in the longer section, was a huge area of rope walls. Several ropes hung from the top of the wall, each rope situated so that a person could climb several different routes. A few auto-belay routes were set for people without partners and were scattered throughout the area. Farther back was a section where people could use their own ropes on what Megan thought she'd heard someone call the "lead walls." With the exception of a few areas, these walls were close to vertical, more or less straight. A thick cushion padded the floor all through the area.

On the right, the smaller section of the V, was the bouldering section, with shorter walls set at a variety of angles. There were sections that looked like caves and sections where a person could even climb, or hang from, the ceiling. In the bouldering area, the floor cushioning was much thicker—almost another foot of padding, Megan thought. This is where people would climb without the ropes. That explained the thicker padding, Megan mused. On the ropes side, the rope would help cushion the fall.

Usually, anyway.

She bit her lip. She wasn't sure where to start.

"You look lost." Brenden was now standing beside her, a friendly smile on his face. Megan noticed one slightly crooked tooth. His nose was slightly too big or too round, maybe, for Hollywood stardom, and his dark curly hair was unruly, peaking at both temples. But his eyes were kind, and his smile was, too.

"I am lost," Megan said. "I don't know where to start."

"Well," Brenden said, "first question: ropes or bouldering?"

Megan realized that Brenden wanted to share his sport with her as a way to help himself cope. She looked again at the ropes, at the tall walls. Shay was over there now, on the wall and being belayed by a woman Megan didn't recognize. Megan knew Edison's staff had gone over the routes and the auto belays, checking bolts and screws and ropes and making sure everything was safe, but she couldn't shake her feeling of unease.

"Bouldering, I think," she said.

"This way," Brenden said. As soon as they were on the thickly padded gray floor, their steps changed and their gait slowed as each foot sunk into the mat, as if they were walking on the moon.

Brenden led Megan to wall with a lower ceiling. "There's also upstairs," he said, pointing to a stairwell Megan hadn't noticed before, back near the lobby and the offices. "The walls up there are a lot shorter so you can't fall as far. But we can start here." He pointed to a label taped to the wall next to a yellow hold.

"Different gyms do it differently, so if you go somewhere else it might change. But here, the grades are taped next to the start hold. Grades start at V0 and in gyms don't go up beyond maybe V11 or V12. Outside, in the whole world there are two V17s, or one V17 and one V16/17, depending on who you ask. One in Finland, and one in France. The 16/17 is France." He looked at Megan to see if he'd lost her.

"Have you climbed the V17s?" Megan asked.

The sudden, short burst of laugh was almost a giggle. "No," Brenden said. "Best I've done is V13, and that was a real project. I'm working on it, though." He placed one hand on the yellow hold. "This hold has the label next to it, and also the same color tape, so you know it's your start hold. Now I'll look around to see if there's another hold with yellow tape next to it. If there were, I'd put one hand on each to start. But there's not, so I'll put both my hands on this hold. Then you just get your feet off the floor onto foot holds, and then you climb. Use only the yellow holds; that's the designated route. You're done when you get to that hold at the top with the yellow tape and touch it with both hands." He quickly scaled the wall, briefly held the top hold with both hands. Then he climbed down a few holds before letting go of the wall and letting himself fall the remaining distance, landing perfectly. "Probably you should down climb for practice," he said. "It's harder and it's good to learn how to do it. Now you try."

Megan placed her hands as Brenden had on the yellow start hold, then shifted her feet to the same foot holds the climber had used. Slowly she moved one hand, then the next, then a foot, then another. Halfway up the wall, she got scared. She felt herself start to panic. How could she be so far off the ground after just a few steps? But the floor already seemed so far away.

"I think I need to come down," she said, her heart beating.

"No problem," Brenden said kindly. "You've got this. Just

climb back down, hold tight but don't over grip. You can use any of the holds on the way back down, not just the yellows."

The holds were slightly rough, and Megan could feel the pull on her skin. This, she realized, was a sport a person would have to ease into. But even through the terror, she felt thrilled. Already she loved it. Slowly and carefully she made her way back to the soft padded floor. And then she wanted to try again.

"This is good for an overthinker," she said, looking back at the route she'd just climbed, assessing where she'd stepped and what hold she could have reached for next. "You really don't think about anything but the wall, the holds. My brain was completely on the wall. I forgot everything else."

"Exactly," said Brenden. "It's a truly zen sport. Climbing is about problem solving. Literally. The routes are sometimes called 'problems.' Your solution, the way you get to the top, is your 'beta.' Try another route."

Megan looked around the walls until she found another route labeled V0, this one pink. She tapped the start hold, but then noticed another hold about two feet away that also had pink tape next to it. "Tape on two holds ... that means I use both holds to start?"

"Quick learner," Brenden smiled.

Megan put one hand on each start hold and lifted her feet onto foot holds, then started climbing. This time she made it a little farther up the wall before she felt nervous again and climbed back down.

"That's exhilarating," she said, a huge grin on her face. "And also exhausting."

"You build up to it. Always be sure you're being safe. You're not in competition with anyone but yourself. Don't go farther than feels safe. It's completely acceptable and normal to climb down like you did, without getting to the top. And be sure to rest between climbs. Like now," Brenden said.

"Getting to the top," Megan said. Her mind stretched back to what Lily had told her when they first got to the gym to be a part of the film. "That's called sending?"

"Exactly," Brenden said. "Sending. Now give yourself a minute to rest."

As Megan sat down on the floor, Brenden found a route he wanted to climb, a black route labeled V9. Compared to the holds on the V0s Megan had climbed, the holds on the V9 were tiny, awkward, and far apart. Yet watching Brenden climb the wall was like watching vertical ballet; as if gravity didn't apply to this man. He glided from hold to hold, occasionally almost leaping from one to the next, hanging under an overhang and then climbing up over a bulge to reach the top hold, again tapping the last hold with both hands before letting go and falling several feet, sticking the landing once more.

The day before, Megan and Lily had watched Bee climb outside while he'd been waiting on the film production crew. Bee had been good, but now Megan understood what people meant when they said Brenden was better. He made it look so easy.

"How long did it take you to get this good?" Megan said as Brenden sat next to her, catching his breath.

"I started when I was four," he said. "A gym went in just outside town and my dad took me to it. I was always climbing on furniture at home, climbing the outside walls up to the roof. They figured it would be safer if I did it in a gym."

"You're good," Megan said. She paused. "You're better than Bee was. Not to disparage the dead. But I can see why you'd be frustrated that he got the lead role."

Brenden stared at a wide green hold high on the wall. "Well, I have it now," he said quietly.

"Heck of a way to get it," Megan said.

Brenden now seemed absorbed in his right shoe, rubbing his thumb against the black rubber of the toe.

"You're clearly passionate about climbing," Megan continued. "Do you find yourself getting absorbed in every aspect of it? Like, knowing all about the different shoes, and all the … I don't know, the different harnesses, different carabiners, whatever. Or learning about route setting, learning the ins and outs of a climbing gym?"

Brenden looked up at the green hold again, then his line of sight seemed to follow the other green holds that led up to it. Squinting, Megan thought she could read the tag next to the start hold: V10.

"Yeah, I guess," Brenden said. "When I'm not climbing I'm reading about climbing or watching videos. But usually I'm planning when I'm going to climb next. The money from this film will be enough that I can dirtbag for a few months at least. Half a year."

Dirtbagging. Owen had mentioned that the day before. "Living in your car?"

"My van. Well equipped," Brenden said. "Better than a hotel."

Megan nodded. "So you've … have you overhauled the inside of the van so you can live out of it? You're good with tools and mechanical things?"

"I can do what I need to do to get done what I need to get done," Brenden said.

Megan tucked this bit of information away.

"I hear they have you staying at the haunted hotel," she said. "How was that? I haven't stayed there. It's pretty new."

"Yeah, it was great," Brenden said, his focus more intent on the green route that he clearly was itching to climb. "They had a special guided tour for us. Then I went to my room and crashed. Long day." He pushed himself up off the thick floor and quickly was on the wall again, climbing up and across and over like he was another creature, a real life Spider-Man.

Megan had brought along a small bag in which to carry her

phone and keys while she climbed, and now, from within the depths of the cloth, she heard her phone buzzing with an incoming text. It was Max.

Max wrote: *Checking in. Any interesting news?*

Megan replied: *I'm at the gym. I've just been talking with Brenden (Donut). Nice guy. I don't get murderer vibes but also he does seem to be resourceful, could have the skills to have done the deed.*

Max wrote: *I'm in the gym parking lot. Are you inside?*

Megan wrote: *Yes. Come on in.*

A figure in the gym doorway blocked the sunlight streaming in. Megan looked up expecting to see Max, but instead it was a man she didn't know. A man who looked tremendously out of place, unless he was planning to change in the gym, but he wasn't carrying a gym bag. He was dressed in a tan suit with a light turquoise shirt and a bolo tie. His dark brown hair, swept back at the forehead, fell almost to his shoulders, and he had a short, neatly trimmed beard and mustache. The man scanned the gym until his eyes fell on Brenden, at which point they lit up with recognition.

"Donut!" the man called out as he walked across the thick mats in his dark brown derby shoes. His tone was too ebullient, too cheerful; both pleasant and condescending, like he wanted to seem friendly but didn't actually care.

Brenden, who was halfway up the wall on yet another route, ignored the man. His focus was on his hands, his feet, the wall, and nothing else as he moved from white hold to white hold. With a final lunge he reached the top hold, and then the top of the wall above it. He hung for a second on the wall, then let himself drop to the mat. Only then did he turn to the man in the suit.

"Hey," he said. He knew the man, but gave away neither disappointment nor delight in seeing him.

"Hey." A deep voice over Megan's shoulder startled her as

she watched the exchange between Brenden and the man. She turned to see Max.

"Hey," she said.

Max nodded at the man in the suit. "Looks like Brenden's agent found him?"

"Ah," Megan said. "That's his agent? I was trying to figure it out."

"Yeah, I met him out in the parking lot. He had some questions about Bee's death. I told him what I could."

"Brenden's agent," Megan said, looking the man up and down again. The suit, the hair, the shoes. The pretense of caring with an underlying aura of nonchalance. The idea that he was from Hollywood made sense. "I guess they have to make a new contract now."

"Probably," Max said. He looked at Megan, noticed the workout clothes, the streaks of chalk dust on her legs from where she'd brushed against the holds. "Climbing today?" he said with delight.

"Yeah, Brenden was showing me the ropes," she said. "Well, not the ropes. The non-ropes. Bouldering. It's so fun. I'm going to have to get a membership. Once all this is … over."

Megan's small bag buzzed again. She pulled out her phone. This time, the text was from Piper.

Hey sorry to bother you. Any chance we can have a second room at the library? Piper wrote.

Megan looked at Max. "It's Piper. She's asking about another bedroom."

Max raised his eyebrows but said nothing.

Megan texted back. *Not a problem at all. For you? Or someone else?*

After a moment, Piper wrote again. For me. Just need some space.

Megan turned the phone so Max could read the texts.

Sure, Megan wrote. *I can be there in fifteen minutes?*

Thanks. I'll wait down at the river, Piper wrote.

"Well, that's interesting," Megan said. She walked to the shoe area to change back into her own shoes. Max followed. "I wonder what's up?"

Max bit his lip and shrugged. Then paused. "Has she said much about us?" he asked, trying to be casual but also looking so vulnerable.

"Not really," Megan said. "She did say that when you dumped her, you said you did it because she had already left."

Max nodded again, slowly. His energy seemed turned in, closed in on himself, making Megan realize that normally, he was quite open. Gregarious. He said nothing.

Megan sat to slip on her street shoes, then put the rental climbing shoes away in their little hole in the wall. "I'm going to wash this chalk off my hands," she said, tilting her head toward the bathrooms. "Then head back to meet Piper. Do you … do you want to come, too?"

Max's eyebrows went up, thinking. After a moment, he nodded once. "Sure," he said. "Meet you there."

When Megan emerged from the bathroom, her hands scrubbed clean of chalk and dirt from the holds, Max was already gone. Brenden was standing next to the wall talking to the man Max had said was his agent. The Assistant Director, Heather Birdsong, had joined them, as had Roman. Brenden seemed agitated, all the energy in his body angling toward the wall, as if the only thing he wanted to do was climb up and away from these people. The agent stood with a big smile on his face that seemed incongruous with the tense stance of his body. Roman's arms were crossed in front of him and he was shaking his head, but his eyes strayed and found Shay on the wall again, and once again he leered. Heather's lips were pursed, her head tilted to such a degree that Megan read it as annoyance.

"I guess negotiations are going well," Megan said to herself.

When she arrived back at the library, she found Max and Piper down at the river at her favorite seating area around the fire pit. Piper had a beer in one hand, the amber-tinted glass bottle sweating in the sunshine. She had pulled her long light brown hair free from its messy bun, and now it pooled gently on her bare shoulders. Max was sitting next to her, but both of them were looking at the river. Megan tried to read the mood of the scene. There seemed to be a weight in the air, but Megan couldn't tell what it might indicate.

On Piper's arm just below her hair a bruise was blooming, which Megan hadn't noticed before.

"Hey," Megan said, settling into a chair on Piper's other side. She pointed to the bruise. "You okay?" Was this bruise the reason Piper needed a room away from Fox?

Piper squinted her eyes in confusion until she figured out what Megan was talking about. "Oh, sure," she said. "From climbing yesterday. I've always got bruises all over." As proof she lifted her capri shorts above her knee to show a wound that had been healing for several days, then a bruise on her shin, then another bruise on her inner thigh above her other knee. "You don't even notice that you bumped something until the bruises show up," she laughed.

"I can imagine," Megan said, rubbing her right knee. "Brenden was showing me how to climb today and my focus was so much on my hands and feet. I think I bumped a hold with my knee, but I'll know more tomorrow." She looked at Max and tried to will him to communicate with her telepathically. Did he want time alone with Piper? Did he want Piper to go away?

"So everything's okay with Fox, then?" Megan said. "I mean, you're not in danger or anything."

"No, no," Piper said. She took a swig of her beer and looked back at the river.

"Last night," Megan continued. "You and Fox were going to run together, but you ended up running separately. What happened?"

Piper stared at the river a little longer before answering. "He forgot he'd made plans," she said.

"Plans?" Megan asked.

Piper still wasn't looking at Megan, or at Max, but her face showed that she was thinking over her answer, making a decision. "He was supposed to meet someone at the speed climbing wall," she said finally.

Megan's mouth dropped for a second before she composed herself. "At the wall," she said, looking at Max. "Who was he supposed to meet there?"

Piper shrugged. "He didn't say."

Megan's mind traced back to earlier, at Rae's pub. "It was Roman's car, though, that you saw at the gym, wasn't it?" she said. "You recognized it at the pub."

Piper pursed her lips. "Well, I suppose it was."

"So was that who Fox was meeting?" Max asked.

This time, Piper's attention was drawn. She looked at Max like she'd forgotten he was there, like she had a thousand questions she wanted to ask. "You'll have to ask Fox," she said. She turned to Megan. "Hey, I'd like to lie down for a bit. Can we get me that other room?" She stood, ready to go.

"Of course," Megan said.

After Megan had settled Piper into a new room on the top floor of the library, she looked out her own balcony to see if Max was still by the fire pit. Seeing that he was, she filled a water bottle for herself and one for Max, then went to join him again.

"Hey," she said, sitting in the chair next to him. She handed him a bottle.

"Thanks," Max said, taking the bottle. He opened the top and took a long drink. "All good?" he said, looking back at the top floor of the library.

"Yeah, she's good." Megan sighed. The rush of the water always seemed to smooth over the rough edges of life. The river at this point was deeper than it looked, she knew. Deep enough to hide secrets, for sure. "Have you ever heard of Ho-ha'-pe? River mermaids? Or technically Water Women, I suppose," she asked. She opened her own bottle of water and took a sip of the cool liquid.

Max laughed, tossing his head back in delight. "River mermaids? No, I haven't. Is there one here?"

Megan watched the river tumbling over boulders, churning the water from clear to white. It was a romantic idea, river mermaids, but it seemed a bit far-fetched. Ocean mermaids made sense; they could live in the deep calm sea, undisturbed by tumultuous currents. "Maybe in calmer rivers," she said.

"I'll keep my eyes open," Max said mischievously.

What Megan wanted to know next, she didn't know how to ask gracefully. "So how well do you think you know Piper?" she said. "I mean, how well did you know her? Do you think you still have a good … do you think you still know who she is?"

One side of Max's lip curled in wry amusement. "What exactly are you asking?" he said. Wrinkles appeared at the corner of his eyes.

Megan shook her head. "I'm not prying," she said. "Not yet. I just mean, is she trustworthy? Would she aid and abet?"

Max looked down river. Searching, maybe, for river mermaids. "Honestly, I don't know." He scanned the river bank on the other side for a while. "In answer to your question," he said, "not the one you asked but the one you didn't ask. In answer to your question, one of the hardest things is realizing that someone just isn't capable of loving you the way you deserve to be loved. Not because you're not lovable but because they don't know how to love." He turned to look at Megan, and his eyes seemed deeper than Megan had ever seen, like she was looking straight through to his heart. "When I knew her, Piper didn't know how to love. And so she didn't really love me. I waited for a while, thinking she might learn, but finally I realized I was just enabling her. Keeping her from having to grow." He paused, looking at his hands. "I realized that she was unreliable, and I'd gotten used to being disappointed. Then I realized that wasn't what I wanted for my life. I know people say you have to set the bar low so you aren't disappointed. I, on the other hand, believe you get what you expect. So I decided to expect more. She couldn't give more. So I left."

Megan bit her lip. This was, in fact, the question she hadn't asked, but she wasn't sure she would ever have asked it. She felt grateful that Max trusted her with this. As she asked her next question, she felt her heart leap into her throat. "Do you think you'd like to get back together with her?"

Max looked at the river again, searching again for that mermaid. "No. It's not like that. We're done. We've both changed. Besides, I have better options now." His eyes crinkled at the edges as he shared a thought with himself. "I think by expecting more, I'm getting more."

Megan's heart thumped. She cleared her throat.

"So I asked the hotel to check their security cameras," Max said, changing the subject, moving on.

"Oh?" Megan said, both disappointed and relieved.

"For comings and goings last night," Max continued. "There were a lot of people in and out, and of course not all of them are associated in any way with the film so I'll be going over the videos myself later. But what they told me was that they have footage of Shay Garrick and Jett, the director who has no last name," Max rolled his eyes, "left about nine. They left at the same time but there's no way to tell if they were heading out together. Shay came back about midnight, and Jett came back about half an hour after that. Roman left at about ten, then returned at about midnight. Other than that, they think most of the film cast and crew were in the hotel."

"Is everyone other than Fox and Piper staying there?" Megan asked.

"Still working on finding out. If you hear anything on that, let me know," Max said.

"Will do," Megan said.

They sat in silence a while, thoughts churning in their minds just as the water churned in the river. The smell of the water always drew Megan to take deep breaths. Crisp. Clean, but in a clean Earth way, not an inside disinfectant way. Healthy. Breathing in the outside air, here by the river, or in the forest, or anywhere outside, really, felt like breathing in wellness. It renewed her. Megan closed her eyes and turned her face toward the sun.

"Oh, shoes," Max said after a few minutes.

Megan opened her eyes and looked at Max. Something seemed more raw about him now. More real. His dark wavy hair was still perfect; his teeth still glistened in the sun. Maybe it was the way he held his shoulders. Less guarded. More open.

"Shoes?" Megan said.

"Piper told me when Fox went for his run, he had his backpack with him. And his climbing shoes."

Megan frowned. "At, what, ten at night? Eleven? Do people climb in the dark?"

Max shrugged. "I mean, some do." He raised an eyebrow. "But it's an interesting piece of information." He looked at his watch and stood. "I need to check back with the station, see what's new. Call me if you find out anything?"

Megan nodded.

"And be safe," Max said. There it was again. That vulnerability to his stance. That openness.

"You, too," Megan said. She watched as the police officer walked away. He had better options now, he'd said.

Well.

Megan headed inside and took the elevator up to her apartment, but halfway up she remembered that the journalist—Georgia Torkelson, Roman's ex-wife—had mentioned that Roman had written several books. When the elevator reached the top floor, Megan turned down the hallway to the door that led down to the library.

Descending the grand staircase from the top floor to the library level of the former mansion always made Megan feel like she was the heroine in her own fairy tale. Only in her fairy tale, she wasn't a helpless damsel waiting to be saved by the handsome prince. In her fairy tale, she was the gatekeeper to countless universes, each world magically accessed by opening a book. In her fairy tale, she wasn't waiting for anyone to rescue her. In her fairy tale, she went out to save others and solve mysteries. With a handsome prince as one of her many quirky, smart, fabulous sidekicks.

At her desk, Megan turned on her computer and waited for the programs to load. As she waited, she took a moment to admire the library. It wasn't her house, of course, but when she had the place all to herself, she almost didn't have to pretend that it was. A dream house, filled with every imaginable book, and upstairs, her rooms, complete with a balcony overlooking the river. She tried, occasionally, to imagine what it would have been like for Edison and his ex-wife. This had been a vacation house for them, but even so it could never have been a home. Whereas as a library it was the perfect refuge for a book lover such as herself, as a vacation house it would have been too loud, too echo-y, too distant for two people.

"Maybe that's why they made it so big," Megan murmured, looking up at the LED fairy lights, hung high on the ceiling, that made the room feel like magic. She tilted her head and noticed the tall walls, as if for the first time. Could she secure climbing holds to those walls? Affix ropes to the top? Could she come down in her off hours and climb on the walls next to the floor-to-ceiling windows by the reading nook that looked out over the river?

No, she wouldn't take business away from River Rock, from Edison.

Still, it was tempting.

A rope, secured to the top of the walls. That was the key, she thought. Who had access to the rope; who had access to the space behind the walls from which they could sabotage the top holds?

And why?

Megan turned to her computer and typed "Roman Shropshire" into the library database. After a moment, the screen came up empty. No search results found.

Megan frowned.

She went to the Amazon website. Maybe Roman's books weren't in her library database, but were on Amazon. "Roman Shropshire," she typed.

Nothing.

"He must have written his books under another name," Megan told the computer screen.

She checked the giant clock on the wall. Just past two in the afternoon. She wasn't hungry but she wanted to know more about Bee.

Time to return to Rae's.

SEVEN

The benefit of a small town, Megan thought as she walked into Rae's, was that there were not a lot of places for people to congregate. If you wanted to find people, there were only so many places to look.

Naturally, Rae's was packed. In a quick look around the room, Megan saw Fox sitting with Brenden, Heather, and the man who was apparently Brenden's agent. Brenden looked somehow uncomfortable and was twiddling his thumbs and jiggling his left leg. Fox's surfer hair looked more unkempt than it had before, and he looked supremely disinterested in the conversation. He was, Megan noticed, sitting quite close to Heather. The agent looked as forced-cheerful as before, and his hair had been swept back into a sleek man-bun. Megan almost laughed, then coughed to cover it up and tried to keep her face neutral.

At another table Shay was sitting with Jett, the director, and Roman. Roman was sitting next to Shay; he was leaning toward her while her body language leaned away from him. Shay's focus was on the counter at the bar and the onion rings she was eating, while Jett and Roman were talking animatedly, hands gesticulating as each made whatever point he needed the other to understand.

Even the journalist, Georgia, was there. Roman's ex-wife. She was sitting alone but her attention encompassed the entire room, as if she were plugged into every conversation, waiting for the right one to focus on.

And in Megan's group's favorite corner table, Edison sat with Owen and Lily. Owen had just said something that made Lily cover her mouth as she laughed; Edison threw his head back and guffawed.

Megan waved at her friends in the corner table, then walked over to Georgia.

"Georgia," Megan said smiling. "Mind if I sit?" Without waiting for an answer, Megan sat.

Georgia smiled a somewhat empty, but not unfriendly, smile. All her tentacles of attention that had been tracking the room snapped back to her own table. "Megan, is that right?"

"Yes, good memory," Megan said. "I can be so bad with names." She caught Rae's eye at the counter and indicated with pantomime that she'd like a glass of water when Rae had a chance.

"Part of the job," Georgia said. "I need to remember details when I'm writing articles."

Megan looked over toward Roman. "Is that how you met? You and Roman?" She realized that not all Georgia's tentacles of attention had pulled back. One was still on her ex-husband.

"In a writing group, yes," Georgia said, her voice dripping with scorn. "Back before he'd published anything. He was working on his first book."

Megan was surprised that the force of Georgia's stare hadn't yet made Roman look over her way. He was definitely engaged in his conversation with Jett. "Were you working on a book, too?" Megan said. "When you were in the writing group?"

Georgia didn't answer immediately. "I was," she said. "But that stopped when I got pregnant."

"Ah," Megan said. "Sorry."

"Stop," Georgia said. "I hate when women say 'sorry' for things they didn't do."

Rae came by with a glass of water and set it down in front of Megan just as Georgia was admonishing Megan. "She's not saying she's sorry for having done it, sweetheart," Rae said, "she's saying she has empathy for the situation and for you in the situation. Don't listen to all those talk show hosts with their pithy advice. We can still be human beings, can't we?" Rae smiled sweetly and walked away.

Megan grinned internally and again tried not to laugh. Rae might be caustic but she would be loyal to her friends to the bitter end.

"I suppose it's my turn to apologize," Georgia said, though it didn't seem like she meant it.

"No worries," Megan said. "Rae is just protective."

Georgia's eyes had drifted back to Roman, whose hand had found its way under the table and onto Shay's leg. "I should probably go save that girl," she mumbled.

But she didn't need to. Without saying a word or giving any above-table indication of what was happening, Shay grabbed Roman's hand and put it firmly back on his own leg. Through the whole interaction, Shay kept strong eye contact with Jett and a smile on her face.

Roman's grin grew wider and he shook his head.

"That's why the marriage ended," Georgia said.

"Because of Shay?" Megan said.

"No, because of all the women," Georgia said. "Especially the ones who didn't refuse. He liked to charm them by telling them he was an author and wanted to write them into one of his books." She rolled her eyes.

"Oh, that reminds me," Megan said. "I looked for him in the library database but couldn't find him. You said he's published?"

"Pseudonym," Georgia said. "He wrote under the name Rowen Shires." She rolled her eyes again.

Megan repeated the name a couple of times in her mind and vowed to look him up when she got back to the library.

"You didn't happen to know Bee, did you?" Megan said, sipping her water. Georgia was almost done with her burger and fries, and Megan didn't want the reporter to get away without asking. "The one who was killed? I'm trying to figure out who knew him."

Georgia's attention snapped back to Megan. "Killed?" she said, raising an eyebrow.

Megan's heart skipped. She'd slipped up. The equipment that had been tampered with wasn't public knowledge yet, apparently.

"I mean who died," Megan stammered. "The climber who died."

Georgia leveled a steady gaze at Megan, then sighed. "I didn't know him. You'll have to ask Roman. I think they all climbed together at one point or another," she said, waving her hand around the room to include the various climbers. "Killed?" she repeated, watching Megan closely.

"Just tragic," Megan said, trying to avoid the subject. She was not a good liar. "I can't believe he decided to climb without a rope."

Georgia's attention was back on Roman, who was now looking back at her, his eyes mocking her. Georgia wiped her lips with her napkin, then pulled out her wallet and placed a ten-dollar bill on the table. "Will this cover it?" she said. She stood and walked away.

"Yup," Megan said to the now empty table. "But just barely."

Megan turned her attention to the table where Fox, Brenden,

Heather, and the agent with the man-bun were sitting. Brenden still looked fidgety. Fox had his arms crossed across his chest; his feet tapped the floor under the table. The agent was talking. Heather was taking small sips of her water and staring out the window. Megan took a breath of courage and headed over.

"Hi," she said to the table, then she turned to the man she hadn't met. "I'm Megan Montaigne. I'm an extra in the film, and also I'm the Library Director here in town." She waved a hand in the general direction of the library.

"And a good friend of Edison Wright," Heather said, without looking at Megan.

The man stood. His smile never seemed to leave his face but also it never seemed to get beyond his lips, Megan noticed. "Troy Langley," the man said. He held out his hand and gave Megan's a firm shake. Then he tilted his head in Brenden's direction. "Brenden's agent."

Brenden's eyes lifted briefly to meet Megan's, as if to acknowledge the statement without giving it any weight.

"Yes, I'd heard," Megan said. "Are you based locally?"

Troy laughed. "Oh, no," he said. "Not at all. L.A. Los Angeles." He added the last bit as if he thought Megan might not know where L.A. was.

"Oh, I though you meant Louisiana," Megan said, smiling at her joke.

No one laughed.

"Um. So have you represented Brenden for a while, then?" Megan asked Troy.

"Just for this film," Troy said. "So far, anyway." He looked over at Brenden. "Have you seen this kid climb? I see a great future. Climbing is all the rage right now. Everyone's doing it. I see a tremendous future."

Fox leaned back and closed his eyes. Megan was sure that underneath his eyelids, his eyes were rolling. She had seen Fox climb a bit the day before, but in all the excitement of being on a film set, and being new to the sport, she hadn't really noticed much about his own abilities. Now she wondered. Was Brenden better than Fox?

"That's exciting," Megan said, looking at Brenden. "He taught me a bit about bouldering earlier. And then climbed the walls like he'd left gravity behind. It was amazing."

"For Brenden, every day is a low gravity day," Troy said. He winked at Megan. "Climbing talk."

Megan nodded. "So do you represent a lot of climbers?" she asked.

"No," Troy said, shaking his head. What would it take for him to shake that smile? It made Megan uncomfortable in how shallow it was. Like a rock skipping across the surface, all the way across a lake and landing on the other side. Never dipping below. "I heard about this project and reached out. I used to do a bit of climbing myself," he said.

"Oh?" Megan said. "Did you know Bee then?"

There it was. The smile, however fake it might have been, dropped. Yet now it was Troy's sorrow that seemed insincere. "Yes," Troy said. "A bit. Good kid. Really … just tragic." He nodded, affirming his own statement. "Tragic."

Brenden looked up again. "They told us at the hotel that it's being investigated as a homicide," he said. Matter of fact. It might have been a question, but it didn't sound like one.

Heather raised her eyebrows and looked at Brenden. "I hadn't heard that?" she said.

"Who told you that?" Megan asked Brenden. She was almost relieved, though. If she'd misspoken with Georgia at least the cat was, apparently, already out of the bag.

Brenden shrugged. "I heard it from Jett. I think he heard it from housekeeping at the hotel. No idea."

This time, Megan picked her words carefully. "Well, they'll want to investigate all possibilities," she said. "I guess that makes sense."

"How'd they do it?" Heather asked. "Has anyone heard?"

Fox leaned forward again. "Cut the rope, and took out a set screw."

Brenden nodded.

Heather's eyes went wide.

"Who would do that?" she asked. "I thought people liked Bee?"

"Good question," Megan said. "Do you know anyone who had an issue with him?" She tried to keep her head from subconsciously turning toward Fox and Brenden.

Heather's eyes shifted to the table where Shay, Jett, and Roman seemed to be getting ready to leave. "No," she said. "Not really."

"He didn't step on anyone's toes, or make unwanted passes at anyone?" Megan asked. "No jealous girlfriends or boyfriends on the scene? Did he owe anyone money?"

Now Heather shifted back in her seat. "No," she said. "I would have noticed, I'd think."

Troy nodded. "It's her job to notice," he said with his Cheshire grin.

"Pretty much everything is my job," Heather said under her breath.

"Which is why it's good that you're good at everything," Troy said, leaning toward Heather with a smile that almost bordered on real.

"Speaking of which," Megan said. "I understand you all are still planning to continue with the filming. If there's anything I can do to help get things on track, let me know. I'm at the library, or pretty much anyone in town knows how to get in touch with me."

Heather's thin lips thinned out again. "That's sweet," she said. "I'll be sure to let you know."

Megan felt certain Heather's "that's sweet" had the same sincerity as the southern "Bless your heart," which she understood meant almost exactly the opposite. "Well," she said. "I'll leave you all to your lunch."

She felt their eyes all watching her as she slipped toward the corner table where her friends were sitting. Somehow she knew she was about to be the subject of their conversation. Which was fine. They were about to be the subject of hers.

"Heyyyy," Owen said, sliding in the seat to make room for Megan. "Solve the murder yet?"

"Not yet," Megan said, sitting. "But at least the word is out that they're looking into it as a possible homicide. I think I was the first to tell that reporter, Georgia, but it sounds like everyone at the hotel already knows."

"Yeah, everybody's talking about it," Owen said.

Edison hung his head for a moment.

"How are you holding up?" Megan asked him. "You know this won't affect River Rock. People know it wasn't the gym's fault."

"Do they?" Edison asked. He shook his head. "I guess one thing in our favor is that there aren't any other gyms around. But this isn't good."

Megan sighed. She knew how hard Edison had worked on this gym, and she was sure he would only employ the most trustworthy people. She vowed to try to figure out a way to promote the gym from the library. There must be books written by climbers, she thought. She'd find those people and bring them in for talks. Clinics at the gym combined with book signings. Something. She'd find a way.

"We were just talking about the gossip we've overheard," Lily said, eyes bright. She was not one to gossip, really, but she was definitely one for gathering information to solve a mystery.

"Oh?" said Megan. "Tell me?"

"Well," said Owen. He glanced over at the table Megan had just left. "Rumor has it that Heather and Fox hooked up at the last filming location."

Megan's mouth formed an O as she inhaled quickly. "Heather and Fox!" And hadn't she just been thinking Fox was sitting mighty close to Heather? Trying to be inconspicuous, she attempted to look at the table out of the corner of her eye. When that didn't work she rolled her head as if stretching her neck, then turned her neck from side to side, lingering slightly when the table with Heather, Fox, Brenden, and Troy was within her view. Was Fox leaning in toward Heather? Or was Heather leaning in a bit toward Fox? She couldn't tell, and the strain was hurting her neck.

"Ah, the old neck stretch," Lily said. "Subtle."

"Whatever," Megan said, looking back at the group at her own table. "Tell me more!"

Owen shrugged. "That's about it," he said. "I overheard it earlier, a couple of people from the film commented on it. One person was speculating whether she'd slept with Bee, and the other said that no, he'd heard it was Fox she hooked up with." He could see the other table more easily from his seat, and he glanced their way now. "Not a matchup I'd have expected, but there's no accounting for taste."

"Whose taste are you questioning?" Lily laughed. "Fox's or Heather's?"

"I'm just saying it must be a case of opposites attracting," Owen said. "Or maybe she just likes bad boys."

"Interesting," Megan said. "Especially interesting that they thought she might have slept with Bee." She strained her eyes again to try to see the table out of the corner of her eyes.

"Get a mirror," Lily said. "Or take a selfie with them in the background."

Megan laughed. "Whatever," she said again. "I wonder. I wonder if Piper found out about Fox and Heather, and if that had anything to do with her moving out of their room."

"Could be," Lily said. "I wouldn't stick around if I were her."

"If it's true," Edison offered. The others looked at him with annoyance. "I mean, we have to be fair. Gossip isn't fact."

"I know," Megan said. "But that's no fun. That part about Bee, though," she said. "If Heather and Bee got together, is there anyone who would be bothered by that? Did Bee have a girlfriend? Does anyone else have eyes for Heather? I wonder if Max has looked into who is sharing rooms with whom at the hotel. Not that that would necessarily tell us anything. People might share just for the sake of costs."

"It's an indie film," Lily said. "I'm sure they're trying to keep a tight budget."

Megan looked at Edison. "You helped fund it, right? Any financial motivations you see anywhere?"

Edison tightened his lips. "I'm one of the primary funders, yes. Sidney Remington helped fund it, too. And they have some big sponsors. Low Gravity Gear, they're a big sponsor."

"Low Gravity Gear?" said Owen.

"They make climbing gear, rock climbing and bouldering equipment, plus all the associated brand stuff. Shoes, jackets, hats, gloves, bags, you name it," Edison said. "But I think you're right. It's pretty low budget, for the most part."

Megan thought a moment about Bee. He had certainly been a handsome young man. Handsome enough that he'd been chosen over Brenden for the lead role, when everyone agreed Brenden was the far better climber.

"Has anyone heard any gossip on Brenden? What's the temperature on him?" Megan asked.

Lily, who also could easily see the other table without having to feign a neck stretch, shifted her glance to the young man. "By all accounts, people seem to like him. I'd say he seems like a nice kid, but quiet."

"Something a little naive about him," Owen said.

"What makes you say that?" Megan said. She was dying for another glance. She scooted closer in the bench toward Owen but still didn't have a good look at Brenden's table.

"Nothing anyone has said, really," Owen said. "You can just sort of tell by his face. He's sweet. He's innocent."

Megan stretched her neck again, this time less subtly. "What?" she said when she returned her neck to its normal position and saw Lily laughing. "Change seats with me then." She turned for a split second to look directly at Brenden. "I mean, I like him, what I know of him. He helped me learn to boulder. Maybe he's Heather's type. She seems commanding, domineering. Maybe she likes someone a little more … meek."

"That would not explain her hooking up with Fox, then," Owen laughed.

"Well, this is getting us nowhere," Megan said. "Unless anyone has anything else to report, Edison, I'd love to go over to the gym and look around the back of the speed climbing wall? Assuming the police are done there."

"They're done," Edison said. He pulled out his wallet and put four twenty-dollar bills on the table. "Tell Rae to keep the change," he said. He turned to Megan. "No time like the present. Let's go."

EIGHT

As Megan and Edison approached River Rock, Megan took a moment to admire the building. Care had been taken to integrate the look of the structure with the environment surrounding it. The shorter climbing wall, of course, had been constructed to look like an actual rock face. The speed climbing wall looked a bit industrial and cold, but that was due to strict guidelines that demanded all speed climbing walls be built in compliance with official specifications in order to qualify for certification. But attention had been paid to the rest of the building, as well. The exterior was painted neither brown nor gray nor forest green but rather a mottled mix of the three that helped it blend into the scenery, a sort of elegant camouflage that had almost a calming effect.

"You've done an incredible job, Edison," Megan said as she parked the car in the front lot. "It's a gorgeous building."

"All credit to the architects," Edison said, but he beamed at the compliment.

Inside, they found Lexi and another staff member elbow-deep in cardboard boxes, giant smiles on their faces.

"What's all this?" Edison said, poking a hand into one of the boxes.

"Low Gravity Gear," Lexi said. "One of the movie sponsors. They sent a ton of gear to the gym. Look!" She pointed to the floor by one wall where heaps of T-shirts, carabiners, harnesses, climbing shoes, bags, ropes, and more were piled. "Soooooooo," Lexi said. She nodded toward the man on her left, the other staff member. "Asher and I were just wondering what you might plan to do with all of this?" Her eyes looked hopeful.

Edison laughed. "They sent it just for our own use?" he said.

"Yeah," Asher said. "They sent a letter." He picked a piece of paper up off the desk and handed it to Edison. Both he and Lexi looked at Edison with great expectancy.

Edison's smile didn't fade as he read the letter. "Sure enough," he said. "I'll tell you what. You two pick what you want, and then I'll figure out what to do with the rest."

"Yes!" Asher said, raising a hand to high-five Lexi. They immediately started digging through the gear, putting aside the equipment they wanted.

"So easy to make some people happy," Edison said to Megan, laughing.

"That's so nice of you," Megan said. "Generous."

"Lexi and Asher have gone above and beyond with the film crew. They deserve it."

The gym lobby door opened and in came a petite woman with short brown hair styled into a pixie cut, her brown eyes wide with frenzy. She stood there for a while, staring at the scene before her as though she couldn't quite comprehend what was happening, but saying nothing.

Finally, Edison stepped in. "Hi. Can I help you with something? We're closed for climbing today, but …"

The woman's gaze shifted to Edison's face, eventually focusing. "Bee," she said, blinking.

Edison's face fell into a look of concern. "I'm sorry. Are you a friend?"

"Where is he?" the woman said. She looked at the pile of gear, and at Asher and Lexi, who had stopped rifling through the equipment to watch this newcomer. "Where is Bee?"

Edison looked at Megan, then back at the woman. "I'm so sorry. Have you heard … What have you heard?"

The woman shook her head. "He fell," she said. Then she paused and looked at Asher and Lexi as if they were aliens. After a few moments she looked back at Edison. "I'm his girlfriend," she said.

Megan's mouth involuntarily formed an O before she caught herself and bit her lip.

"I'm so sorry," Megan said. "We can't … I can give you the number for the police station. They can tell you more." She turned to Lexi and Asher. "Do you guys have a pad of paper and pen I can use?"

Asher popped up from his spot by the open boxes on the floor, and grabbed the requested materials from a cubby hole in the desk. He handed them to Megan, his eyes wide.

Megan looked closely at the paper. It had occurred to her that the note she'd found in the parking lot could have been written on a pad of paper from the gym. But if that was the case, it wasn't this pad. The paper she'd found in the lot had been white, plain, about three inches by four inches, she guessed. What Asher handed to her was a small yellow legal pad, five inches by eight inches. She frowned, then pulled out her phone to get the number for the police station. Caution told her not to give this woman Max's direct number.

After writing down the number, Megan ripped the sheet from the pad and handed it to the woman. "Here you go. I'm Megan, by the way. What's your name?" she said.

"Caitlyn," the woman said, squinting at the numbers like she couldn't figure out how to read them. "Caitlyn Sheppard."

"I'm so sorry for your loss, Caitlyn," Megan said. "Did you just get into town? Did you drive yourself here?" Catilyn's state of mind had Megan a little concerned, and she didn't necessarily want someone so distracted driving the streets of Emerson Falls.

Caitlyn's focus shifted to Megan from the sheet of paper in her hand. "I have a hotel room …" she said. Then she turned and left.

"Wow," Edison said after Caitlyn was well out of earshot. "She's not doing so great."

"No," Megan said, still frowning. "I'm worried about her. I wonder which hotel she's at? Maybe I should check in with her." Her musings were mostly to herself.

"Not a bad idea," Edison said.

Megan still had her phone in her hand. She started tapping out a message. "And probably I should let Max know she's here." After a few moments, she hit "send," then put her phone back in her pocket. "Well, I guess that's that for now. Should we …?" She tilted her head in the direction of the speed climbing wall outside. She wanted to get inside the back of the wall and see what, if anything, was there to be seen.

Edison looked at the stack of T-shirts with the Low Gravity Gear logo on them. "Save me a large," he said to Asher. "And save a shirt for Megan, too." He smiled at Megan. "Follow me," he said.

They edged around the front desk to a door that led back to the offices. They wove through desks and shelves of gear and holds not in use and the office bathrooms and a staff break room before arriving at yet another door. When Edison opened it, there was almost a physical change in the air. The doorway opened into a narrow, dark space that had an aura of great volume. Edison flipped a switch on the wall. Instantly the space was illuminated. Megan stepped gingerly through the doorway and looked up, hearing her steps echo all the way to the top.

They were in the space behind the speed climbing wall.

"Wow," Megan said. "It's tall." The entire area was only about four feet wide and twenty feet long; a series of ladders and platforms ascended up to the top, more than fifty feet above. Megan felt that even her thoughts might echo within this space.

"After you," Edison said.

Megan put a foot on the lowest rung of the first ladder and reached up with her hand. "I think I prefer bouldering to ladders," she said. The platforms spaced at intervals up the ladders were not solid but rather steel bars woven together so a person could see through them. The first such platform wasn't that far up, but Megan nonetheless clung tightly to the metal as she climbed. When she got to the platform she breathed a small sigh of relief. "We're going all the way to the top?" she said, looking up.

"All the way to the top," Edison said, climbing up behind her.

Megan got back on the ladder and continued climbing until she was at the top platform. The chances of falling down to the bottom were very low, but Megan decided it would be better not to look down. Shortly, Edison popped his head through the opening in the last platform, and then climbed through. He leaned over and flipped a section of the grate over the hole they'd climbed out of, essentially sealing the platform and making it whole.

Megan looked down through the open grate all the way down to the floor far below. "Hellooooooooo down there," she said. Even though she's spoken quietly, her voice echoed around them. "So this is where a person would have gained access to the outside?" She looked around for a window.

"Yeah," Edison said. "Police have already been through here, in case you were concerned about adding your fingerprints." He clicked a latch on the wall and slid open a panel. A gust of fresh air blew in. "Voila," Edison said.

The panel, maybe two feet wide in each direction, was at about chest level. Handles on three sides of the panel offered stability; Megan grabbed the one on the side and the one above the panel, then poked her head out of the open space.

"Wooooooahh," she said. The view before her was breathtaking. From this vantage point, more than fifty feet off the ground, she could see up and down the Skagit River. From this height the sound of the water rushing by was diminished to a whisper; the ripples were smoother and the flow seemed more serene. Megan felt the force of water in her soul, like a calling. Water was her element. Her eyes drank it in.

Gripping the holds extra tight, Megan looked down and to the right, to the west. Below her she could see a runner on the riverfront walk, a woman with a ponytail that bounced and flipped with her stride. Another person was walking in the opposite direction and Megan watched as the two exercisers nodded in acknowledgement of each other without stopping. She looked farther west. "There's Addie's Park," she said, noticing that her favorite bench from which to watch the river flow by was empty. Megan then turned her head to the left, past the town limits, toward Edison's home. "Can't quite see your house," she said.

"By design," Edison laughed. "You think I want people peeping in my windows?"

Megan craned her head to the right again, leaning out the window a bit farther. "I can't see the library, though." She pulled her body back in and immediately felt enclosed in the space. "You should put windows on every wall up here. What a view!"

"Exactly what I need," said Edison. "As if this hasn't caused enough trouble."

Megan nodded, remembering their mission. She looked out the window again, this time keeping her focus close. "I see the holds here," she said. She reached an arm out the window, and felt Edison protectively grab the waistband of her jeans. She turned her head to smile at him. "Don't get fresh," she said. Edison raised his eyebrows inquisitively. "I'm just kidding," Megan laughed. "Please hang on to me. Would a person normally be clipped in up here?"

"A person wouldn't normally be up here," Edison said. "But yes. All precautions, always. It's obviously pretty safe, but we don't want any more accidents."

"Or non-accidents," Megan said. She leaned out again and reached for the top hold on the speed climbing route on her left. "I can reach this one," she said, "and I can reach the top of the auto belay. Both pretty easily." She then shifted toward the right. "But I can't reach the other route," she said.

"There's another opening," Edison said. Megan pulled herself back inside and saw a second panel farther to the right, latched like this one had been, with the same steadying handles on three sides.

"So someone would have had to reach out and unscrew the set screws from here?" she mused out loud. She leaned her head out the panel again, pretending to hold a drill in her hand. She clung tightly to one of the handles and squatted a bit to maintain her balance. "It's definitely possible but it's not something I'd want to do without some safety precautions."

"The panels are mostly to access the top of the auto belays," Edison said. "The routes are generally set from the outside and then left alone. But yes, a person could do it from here."

Megan looked straight down. "You'd think a person would be pretty conspicuous if they did it, but I guess maybe not. People don't always look up. And with the river right there, it might have covered up the sound, or at least blended it in. When was the security camera off again?"

"From shortly before the film crew wrapped for the day until about an hour before Bee showed up," Edison said.

"So it wasn't even after everyone was gone," Megan said. She looked down below again. The film crew trailers were around the other side of the building, as was most of the parking lot, though there were a few spots out front. The entrance to the gym was below and to her left, and then the other arm of the building led to the shorter wall, the one that blended in so well with the surroundings.

"A person on that wall might have been able to see someone up here," she said, pointing.

"On the Northwest Face?" Edison said. "That's what it's called, that wall. The Northwest Face. Like the North Face, on the Eiger mountain in the Swiss Alps, but Northwest." He grinned at his cleverness.

"It's not just a clothing brand? North Face?" Megan asked.

"It's a clothing brand named after a famous face of a mountain," Edison laughed. "Regardless, when you're on the Northwest Face, chances are you're not looking this way. You're focused on the wall, or maybe looking out to the right at the river. But probably not up here."

"Probably not, but not definitely not," Megan said. "Was anyone climbing this wall yesterday, during shooting, late in the day?"

Edison frowned, trying to remember. "I don't think so," he said. "I think they may have been getting it set up for shooting. There are actually panels at each of the platforms, below." He pointed down the ladders to the steel platforms beneath them. "They were going to use them to film out of."

"Who would have had access then?" Megan asked.

"Well, the whole film crew, really," Edison said. He shook his head. "I did not think this would turn out this way."

Megan put a hand on Edison's arm. "Hey. You couldn't have known. This isn't on you." She felt a surge of anger for whoever had put her friend in this position, followed by a surge of determination. "Okay. The cameras were off before the end of the filming day. Crews may have been in here. We should ask around and see if anyone was on the Northwest Face. Maybe they noticed something. And then as for cutting the rope down at the bottom," she leaned out the window again. "I suppose anyone could have done that, too."

"Square one," Edison said.

"Square one," Megan said, "but that's never stopped me before." She slowly dropped to the floor and sat with her back to the wall.

Edison did the same.

"Edison," Megan said after a moment. "You've been around these people for a while now. What do you think of each of them?"

Edison shrugged. "Give me a name. Where to start."

Megan thought. "Okay. Fox."

Edison nodded, thinking. "Okay. Fox. To be honest, not the deepest guy. What you see is what you get. He's a stereotype of himself, right down to the surfer looks and the matching attitude. A bit of bravado. Likes to be the center of attention. Likes to be seen. Doesn't like to be shown up. Competitive. Likes to be seen with the right people. Maybe a bit manipulative."

"Hmm," Megan said. "Brenden?"

"Brenden," Edison said, stroking his chin. "Brenden is more sensitive. A little naive. I think he's got a crush on Shay. Or at least he's a little protective of her. Great climber, doesn't really care about others' climbing. Stays in his own lane. Honest. Not showy."

"Bee?" Megan prompted.

Edison sighed. "He was a good kid. Also competitive. Definitely wasn't staying in his own lane."

"What do you mean?" Megan asked.

"I mean, he cared way too much about … about image. About winning, and getting ahead. I think that's part of why he didn't climb as well as Brenden. He wasn't climbing for himself. He was climbing to impress. The whole climbing late at night without a rope? That's ego. You can use a rope without relying on a rope. He wanted to impress. He was more concerned with other people than his own sense."

"But it wasn't climbing without a rope that killed him," Megan said. "Everything was tampered with."

Edison shrugged. "Still."

Megan nodded. "Okay. Um … Piper." She cleared her throat involuntarily.

"Piper," Edison said, the edges of his lips tilting up in amusement. "You tell me?"

Megan rolled her eyes. "No, you tell me."

"I haven't gotten to know her much. She seems nice." He looked Megan in the eyes, watching for her reaction. "Do you think Max would have dated someone who wasn't nice?"

Megan sighed. "Well, I wouldn't think so. But people change. You know. You're young, you make mistakes, you date the wrong people, you grow, you move on."

Edison shifted his legs. "I can't argue with that. Having been married to … to Daphne." He paused. "Speaking of which, there's something about Heather."

"Heather?" Megan said. "Okay. Heather."

"Yeah, Heather. Something familiar about her. Like I know where she's been. Or she knows where I've been."

"You mean an abusive relationship?" Megan asked.

"Yeah," Edison said. "I'm not sure. There's just something."

"I don't know," Megan said. "She seems sharp."

"Sharp smart?" Edison asked. He lifted the grate that was covering the opening by the ladder, then let it down again.

"Well, yes," Megan said. "But also sharp pointy. Edgy. Causing edginess."

"I can see that," Edison said. "Both assessments. I think she's super smart. I was watching her on set and she seems like the type who can figure out anything. But the edginess, I don't know. Maybe that's self protection."

Megan scratched her shoulder. "I suppose. Could be. Okay. Ummmm … Roman."

Edison nodded again. "Yeah, Roman. I think he thinks he's pretty grand," he said. "Pretty impressed with himself. But maybe that's all bravado, too."

"I talked with his wife a bit. She is less than impressed with him," Megan said. "Which reminds me, she said he wrote some books under a pseudonym. I have to look those up when I get back to the library. I'm quite curious."

"He did? What kind of books?" Edison asked.

"No idea," Megan said. "I'll let you know. All right. Who else. Uh … Well, Shay."

"Shay," Edison said. "Shay comes off as quiet but she's pretty badass. She's set some climbing records, but you'd never know it if you had to wait for her to tell you. Now that I think about it, she and Brenden might make a good team. Hmm."

"Hmmm, indeed," Megan said. She leaned and bumped shoulders with Edison. "Look at you, Mr. Matchmaker."

"My talent knows no ends," Edison said, grinning.

"What about Jett?" Megan said. "Speaking of quiet. What do you think of him?"

"Yeah, totally quiet," Edison said. "But you can tell he's always thinking. I've been watching him, too. He won't say anything for minutes and then out of nowhere he has this idea you'd never have thought of but which is perfect. Attention to detail. Creative thinker."

"What about his relationship with the others?" Megan asked.

"Well, I've seen him with Shay," Edison said, "but as far as I know that's just friendship."

"Does he get along with the actors? With Roman?" Megan asked.

"I haven't seen any conflict," Edison said. "But like we said, he's a quiet one. Maybe he's a slow burner."

Megan stretched her legs. "Well. Much to think about. It would be really helpful if the murderer had spray painted something on these walls up here. Alas, our search continues." She stood and offered Edison a hand up, then peeked out the window one last time, breathing in deeply the fresh summer air. "You know, this would be a good date spot up here. A tiny table, a bottle of wine, and a million dollar view. You could make money off this."

"I don't need money," Edison said. "But I'll keep the date idea in mind. Where are you off to now?"

"The library," Megan said. "Time to find out what Roman Shropshire, a.k.a. Rowen Shires, has to say."

NINE

It was Sunday so the library was closed. Megan loved the library patrons; she knew she might be biased but it seemed to her that people who liked to read or research, and especially people who visited the library, were probably the nicest, smartest, most interesting people in the world. Nonetheless, she also savored her time alone in the library and loved having the whole space to herself, to use for her own purposes. She started out with the intention of going to her desk, but a sunbeam streaming in through the floor-to-ceiling windows by the reading nook diverted her, as if she were a cat, required by nature to sit a moment and soak in the rays. Heeding the call, Megan sat down in one of the overstuffed chairs, first slipping her shoes off and tucking her feet underneath her. The flow of the river outside made her think of order. Things might seem chaotic, but there was always a reason. Nothing happened without a reason. All she had to do was find it.

And, she thought, she also needed to get someone in to wash those windows. While the river spoke to her of order, the sunbeam on the windows spoke to her of dirt.

"Note to self," she said out loud to the windows. "Call in the window washer."

Megan checked her phone, though she hadn't heard or felt any notifications. She wondered a moment about Max and Piper. And Piper and Fox. Was Piper only attracted to men whose name ended in an x? And if so, what did that say about her?

"I think this sunbeam is frying my brain," Megan said to the sunbeam.

With a sigh, she heaved herself out of the chair and slipped her shoes on before veering back on course to her desk. She sat with her chin cupped in her hand as she waited for her computer to boot up and for her database to load.

Finally the flashing curser floated on her screen.

"Rowan Shires," Megan said out loud as she typed the name into the search engine.

This time, her search was successful. Several titles popped up on the screen, published over the last decade. All were listed as murder mysteries.

The titles made Megan's eyes pop.

> *Death on the Rocks*
> *Offed on the Ropes*
> *The Problem with Murder*

Rocks. Ropes. And a bouldering route, Megan remembered, was sometimes called a problem.

Were these books about rock climbing murders?

A chill spread through Megan as she clicked through to read the description of *Death on the Rocks*:

The rock climbing community is reeling: while attempting first ascent of an epic route, one of their most beloved climbers tragically falls to his death. But things turn even darker when suddenly it appears the tragedy may not have been an accident after all. Who could have wanted the famous climber dead? And will the mystery be solved before the murderer takes another victim?

"He writes murder mysteries about … rock climbing?" Megan said in disbelief to the computer. She clicked through the descriptions of the other books and sure enough, every one of them centered on the murder of climbers.

Megan leaned back in her chair, her mouth hanging open, her eyes squinted in confusion as she stared at the screen.

"That's got to be a coincidence," she said, but she didn't believe it even as she said it. It wasn't unheard of for murder mystery authors to act out their own novels. Or was that just urban legend? Was she making it up? Was she being gullible?

Megan pulled up a browser and searched: *murder mystery writers who commit murder*. The list wasn't long, but there was indeed a list.

Was there a new murder mystery author to add to the case files?

Megan pulled out her phone and tapped out a text to Max: *FYI. Might be nothing. Roman Shropshire has written murder mysteries under the name Rowen Shires. All seem to be about rock climbing murders.*

Max didn't reply. "Must be out saving people," Megan said to herself as she watched her phone.

She then wrote out a message to Edison: *Have you seen Roman? Is he around?*

Edison wrote back quickly. *I think he's here at the gym somewhere. Just saw him a few minutes ago. Do you want me to get him?*

No worries, Megan replied. *I'll come back.*

"I really do need to get a membership at the gym," Megan muttered to herself as she headed to her car. "Seems I'm spending all my time there!"

The film set area outside the gym wasn't buzzing like before, but it also wasn't completely empty when Megan returned. She stopped the nearest person with a headset and a clipboard.

"Excuse me, you working on the film?" Megan said.

The woman nodded.

"Do you know if Roman is around?" Megan asked.

The woman pointed toward the back of the gym. "In his trailer," she said. "It's the biggest one on the end." She went back to her clipboard.

Megan nodded her thanks and walked briskly around the building. She hadn't taken much time before to check out the back lot, as it were, where several trailers had been set up for the primary cast and crew. An arrow on a sandwich board that said "CATERING" pointed toward one end where a trailer and a canopy with several tables were set up, around which a few people were milling about, plates in hand. On the other end several trailers were bunched together. One of them was slightly bigger than the others. Megan headed there first.

As she approached the trailers she could see placards outside each door. "FOX" was right next to "BEE." Megan felt a lump in her throat as she passed by Bee's trailer. She assumed Max had already been in there to see if anything struck him as odd. Maybe she'd ask if she could go in, too.

After Fox and Bee's trailers were several longer trailers with two or three doors each, segmented to house more actors in a smaller space, Megan imagined. "Indie budget," she said to herself. These, too, had placards. "BRENDEN" was next to "SHAY." "PIPER" was on the next trailer down.

At the very end Megan found the trailer she was looking for, identified with a placard that said "ROMAN." The trailer, nondescript on the outside, was about twenty feet long and maybe eight feet wide with a popout section on the right. The popout section extended three feet away from the main part of the trailer to create more space on the interior. Six steel steps led up to the narrow door near the left end, and on the other side of that was another popout section. Megan climbed the steps and knocked, suddenly feeling a little nervous.

"Hello?" she called out. "It's Megan Montaigne."

Something inside the trailer bumped, and then Megan heard Roman's voice call out. "Come in!" he said. "I'm indecent!"

"Sorry?" Megan said tentatively. "Should I come back?"

More thumping came from inside the trailer, then the door opened with Roman smiling wide, almost leering. He was sweaty, dressed in running shorts. He'd taken off his T-shirt and now wore it draped around his neck like a towel. "I'm indecent," he said, "but you're still welcome. I'm just back from a run. Eight miles. Gorgeous out there. Come on in."

Megan quickly took in her surroundings. She'd never seen a film crew trailer before but she'd heard stories of the movable mansions some top-tier actors commanded when they were on set. This one was much more humble. As she walked in, the bathroom was directly in front of her. To the left she could see a bedroom with a rumpled bedspread and clothes tossed on a chair.

"This way," Roman said, watching her look into the bedroom. He led her the other direction, past the bathroom and into an area with couch seating on the right and a small kitchenette and kitchen seating on the left. At the very end of the trailer was a workspace and chair. Roman's laptop sat on top of the table, along with several framed photographs and a fresh vase of flowers. "They bring me fresh flowers every day," Roman said, noticing her gaze. "Perks of being a producer I guess. Have a seat."

Megan sat on the unexpectedly comfortable couch next to the workspace. The trailer's interior wasn't fancy, but it was fancier than she had thought it would be. It was decorated with a subtle but classy touch, and a clean, minimalist look. The bouquet of flowers brightened the space considerably. "They're lovely," Megan said.

Then her heart skipped a beat. Next to the laptop was a folded piece of paper, slightly open so she could almost make out what was written inside.

The paper looked exactly like the paper she'd found outside, in the parking lot. The part she could read said "Meet me …"

"… Some lemonade?" Roman said, startling Megan out of her thoughts.

"Um?" Megan blinked, trying to catch up to the conversation that apparently had been going on without her. Roman was holding up a pitcher of lemonade and a fresh glass, eyebrows raised. "Oh. No, thanks," she said.

"They bring me lemonade, too, when I go on a run," Roman smiled. He poured himself a tall glass and drank it down before coming up for breath and refilling it to the top. "Good people." He draped his T-shirt on the seat of one of the kitchen chairs, then sat on it. "How can I help you today?"

"First, I'm so sorry about Bee," Megan said. Roman's face changed almost immediately, as if he'd forgotten he was supposed to be upset.

"Oh, right. Terrible. Yes, your police have been all over." He frowned.

"A good opportunity for Brenden, though," Megan said. "Horrendous way to get an opportunity, but a good opportunity nonetheless."

Megan felt a shift in the room as the producer's guard went up. "Terrible," he said. "Terrible." He took another long gulp of lemonade, ice clinking in his glass.

"Brenden seems like a good kid," Megan continued, and she felt Roman's demeanor ease a tiny bit. Her mind shifted back to that note on the table next to her. Did it match the one she'd found in the parking lot? If only he'd go into the other room, she could look quickly and see.

"He's a good kid," Roman said. "Maybe too good for his own good."

"What do you mean?" Megan asked.

Roman shrugged and stared deep into his glass of lemonade.

"He's quite trusting," he said finally.

"A good climber, though," Megan said.

"An excellent climber. Far better than I'll ever be," Roman replied. He finished off his second glass of lemonade and poured himself another.

"Yes, I heard someone mention that you climb. I also talked to your wife. Ex-wife, I mean. She told me you wrote some books. I looked them up," Megan said.

Roman turned very slowly toward Megan. "They're under a pseudonym," he said.

"Yes," Megan said. "Rowan Shires. *Death on the Rocks. Offed on the Ropes. The Problem with Murder.*"

Roman curled his lips around his teeth and raised his chin. "Interesting," he said. "You've looked them up."

"They're murder mysteries about climbing," Megan said.

"Yes, they are. A lot of people write murder mysteries."

"A person might think that was an unusual coincidence," Megan said. She was watching Roman carefully but he was keeping his thoughts and movements close, staying rock-still.

He popped his eyebrows slightly. "A person might," Roman said. "But if a person is insinuating that a person who wrote a book about murder is necessarily a murderer, a person might want to be careful. Slander and whatnot." He tilted his head quickly and caught Megan's eyes with his own, holding them in lock. "I suppose you've told your police friend?" Roman said.

"I have," Megan said.

"Well, then, your police friend will get to the bottom of this. I need to shower and get on with my day, I'm sorry you have to leave so soon." Roman stood and swept an arm toward the door, indicating that Megan should leave.

The note, she thought. The note is still on the table. I need to get that note.

But there was no chance, now. Feeling the tension in the room rising, Megan decided it would be best to leave.

On her way to her car, Megan texted Max:

Appetizers and cocktails by the river tonight? 6:30?

Max texted back:

It's a date. See you then.

Megan took care of some work in the library for a couple of hours, then returned to her apartment to fix a picnic for herself and the police officer. She mixed up a shaker of margaritas and poured it into a thermos, pulled some brie out of the refrigerator and scrounged for crackers, washed some red grapes, cut up some carrots, grabbed some dip, and put it all in a large tote bag along with utensils and napkins and plastic glasses and a tablecloth. At the last minute she added a bottle of a red blend to the tote, along with a wine opener. On her way out the door she saw her sunglasses, and she tossed them into the bag as well.

She was just getting the picnic spread out when she heard a car coming around the back of the library. Max.

"Hey!" she called out to him once he was within hearing distance. Out of uniform, she noticed. He always looked particularly nice out of uniform, she thought. Not that he didn't look nice in uniform. But out of it he just seemed … more approachable, maybe. More real.

Megan poured margaritas for herself and Max out of the thermos and held one up for him. He settled into a chair next to hers and took the drink.

"Cheers," Max said, clicking his plastic glass to Megan's.

"Cheers," Megan said.

They both leaned back into their wooden seats and watched the river flow by for a while. A small branch had fallen off of a tree somewhere upstream and was making its way down the river, bumping into rocks and bobbing up and down as it blazed along on its adventure. It got snagged for a few moments on a small boulder, but then triumphantly escaped and continued on downstream.

"This is the life," Max said. "I swear that water makes my heart rate slow, just by watching it."

"Same," said Megan. She watched the branch until it was out of sight.

"One of the best spots in Emerson Falls," Max said. "Next to the falls themselves, maybe."

"I guess Edison and his wife knew what they were doing when they bought this land. But I'm glad they gave it back to the town. Well, glad he did. I don't imagine Daphne would have."

"Fact," said Max. He took another sip of the drink and closed his eyes.

Megan watched him for a minute. Max was so calm, so easygoing, even in emergencies. Had she ever seen him flustered? Well, maybe a few times. But in general, whatever happened, he took it in stride. A good quality for a cop, she thought.

His eyes were still closed when he finally broke his silence. "So did you learn anything today?" he asked casually.

A fish jumped in the river, disappearing so quickly Megan wondered if she'd even seen it.

"Yeah, a couple of things," she said. "Edison showed me the inside of the speed climbing wall, but I know you guys already covered that." She glanced at Max. He was nodding gently.

"Also I had an interesting conversation with Roman," Megan continued. At this, Max opened his eyes and turned his head in attention.

"Oh?" he said. He took a sip of the margarita. "This is perfection, by the way," he said, licking his lips.

"Thank you. It's a mix, but I'll take credit," Megan said. "Yeah, Roman's ex-wife had told me that he wrote some books. I looked earlier but didn't find anything. I saw her today and she told me his pseudonym so I looked it up."

"And?" said Max.

"And he writes, or at least wrote, murder mysteries," Megan said.

Max shifted to look more directly at Megan. "Oh?" he said. "Interesting." His eyes glazed over a bit as he contemplated the ramifications of this new information.

"Murder mysteries about rock climbing," Megan continued.

Max sat up, his attention caught. "Very interesting. Anything like the situation we're looking at here?" he asked.

"I haven't read them yet," Megan said. "That's on the agenda for tonight."

Max leaned back again. "Well, let me know."

"I will," Megan said. "Anyway, I went and talked to him about it."

Max sat up, eyebrows raised. "Alone? Was this before or after you knew about the murder mysteries?"

Megan rolled her eyes defiantly. "After. But I was safe."

Max shook his head. "If you're going to do that sort of thing, which I know you are, can you please at least tell me? So I can identify your body if I need to?"

Megan laughed. "Okay fine. Anyway, the thing is, on official business, do you think you can get into his trailer?"

"His movie set trailer?" Max said. "Not really. Not officially. I have to have more to go on than the fact that he's a writer. Not every writer is a murderer."

"Yeah, but it's not just about the books, though," Megan said. "While I was in there …"

"Alone in the trailer of someone you thought could be a murder suspect," Max said pointedly.

"Or not a suspect," Megan said. "Not every writer is a murderer, you know. Anyway, there was a note on his desk. On paper that looked an awful lot like the paper I found in the parking lot. And it was folded, but I could still see the words 'MEET ME' written on the inside."

"Hmm," said Max. "That is interesting. But again, not enough bring him in on, by any means. You didn't get a picture or anything?"

"He may have kicked me out before I had a chance," Megan said.

Max shook his head, somewhere between amused and annoyed out of his concern for her. "Maybe I can go in and ask him some questions," he said. "See if he'll invite me in. But again, there's not much to go on."

Max's eyes darted to his left and his focus shifted into the distance. Megan turned to see what had caught his attention and saw Fox, watching them as he walked toward the river.

Fox saw the drinks in their hands and smiled. "Hey, bartender! Got more of those?"

Megan smiled. "Sorry, I didn't bring more glasses. Do you want some?"

"Nah," said Fox. He stopped a few feet away from them, hands on hips. "Gotta stay in shape now that I'm single again. I'm assuming Piper told you? When she asked for her own room? She blew it all out of proportion, I'm sure."

"Told me what?" Megan asked. The setting sun was bright in her eyes and she put up a hand to shield them.

"About Heather," Fox said. "Look, Heather seduced me. Not the other way around. Who was I to say no to the Assistant Director? Could have ruined my career." He smirked, and a soft breeze lifted his hair. "It was some of that Hollywood scandal stuff. They don't believe you when you're the guy, though." He winked at Max. "Right, sailor? You hear me. The ladies can't stay away sometimes. They want to test out my eight pack." He patted his stomach. "I'm the victim here." The twinkle in his eye suggested he did not entirely feel like a victim.

Megan felt a wave of compassion for Piper and was glad she'd distanced herself from Fox, whatever her reason might have been. "Were you and Heather together long?" she asked.

"Nah. Just a few times. Pretty long each time, though." Fox winked at Max.

Max nodded in weak acknowledgment, but behind the nod Megan definitely thought she could sense his less-than-impressed opinion of Fox.

Fox shot finger guns at Max and Megan. "You kids don't get into too much trouble, eh?" he said, then he jogged off toward the library.

Megan shook her head. "Don't get into too much trouble, please, Max? I know how you like to stir things up."

"Same with you," Max said. He eyed the thermos. "Any more margarita in there?"

Megan poured the last drops into Max's glass. "But don't worry, there's wine," she said, pointing to the basket she'd brought down. "I can't believe Piper went from dating you to dating Fox," she said.

Max let out a chuckle. "She probably dated a few in between," he said.

"A quick slope downward, apparently," Megan said.

"Who knows," Max said. "People change over time. I haven't seen her in years. Maybe she's changed."

Megan drained the last bit of her margarita, and then opened the wine and poured herself a glass. "That's true. I mean … I don't know if this will sound insensitive, but if it does … well. I mean Zeus and me," she said, referring to her fiancé, who had died in a plane crash. "I'm not sure I'd date him again if I met him now."

Max nodded slowly. "Oh?" he said, leaving the conversation wide open for Megan to take it wherever she felt comfortable.

"Yeah, it's just … I think I got engaged to him because he wanted to. I'm not sure I wanted to. Don't get me wrong. He was a great guy. I just know … I've changed."

Max looked at Megan for a long time without speaking, but his eyes seemed to be reading her like a story. Finally, he raised his glass. "Well. Here's to change," he said.

Megan smiled widely. Zeus had been a good man. She missed him. But there were still many good men around. "To change."

TEN

The next morning, Megan awoke with a smile on her face and a feeling of contentment. She couldn't remember her dreams, but the aura of them still lingered. Happiness. Softness. Togetherness. Someone. She thought she knew who the someone was, but as happens in the fleeting moments after awakening, every detail was soon gone.

"Hello, morning," she said, yawning and stretching as she admired the sky outside her bedroom window, already a bright blue. Clarity, she thought. Bright blue skies felt like clarity. Like progress. This was going to be a good day.

She and Max had kept company with the wine and the evening sky only until about twilight, at which time Max had declared he needed to get home. Megan spent the rest of her evening digitally flipping through Roman's books. She was still not sure of what to make of the similarities. As far as she could tell, none of the murders matched the exact scenario they were dealing with at River Rock, but one book did mention a rope that had been tampered with, and another centered on the malfunction of an auto-belay device. Megan had gone to bed hoping her brain would come up with some answers, but she'd had no such luck. If her brain had absorbed any clues, the puzzle pieces were not coming together.

After a shower and a nice cup of coffee out on her balcony, Megan headed down the grand staircase into the library. The library wouldn't open until noon but there was plenty to do in the meantime. She busied herself with paperwork, and then after an hour or so decided to spend some time re-shelving books. The orderliness of the process always seemed to put her own mind in order, too, and allowed for thoughts in the back of her head to percolate until the moment of insight. Of clarity.

A cart of biographies and nonfiction books was sitting in the office area, sorted and ready and waiting to be put back on the shelves. Megan pushed it out onto the floor and into the biography section. She traced her finger along the spines of the books to find the correct space for Angelou, Maya: *I Know Why the Caged Bird Sings*. "Such a good book," Megan whispered to the shelves. "Good call, whoever checked this out." She shelved a few more books, then came to Caldwell, Tommy: *The Push*. "Insane," Megan said to the book, mesmerized by the cover photo of a man clinging inconceivably to an almost vertical rock wall. "How is that even possible?" Tommy Caldwell, she knew from studying up to be an extra in the movie, was a famous rock climber with a truly unbelievable background story, the kind an editor would reject as "too far-fetched." It involved a kidnapping while rock climbing in Kyrgyzstan and, separately, an incident with a table saw in which he cut off much of his own index finger and his subsequent struggle to return to rock climbing—from which he emerged stronger and better than ever. As she made space for the book on the shelf, she stopped and looked again at the cover. "Maybe I'll read you," she said to the book, and she put it back on the cart. "I wonder who had checked that out?" she murmured before moving on to shelve the next book.

Megan was down to the L section of the biographies when she felt her phone buzz in her pocket. She checked the screen: a text from Max.

You inside? he wrote.

Inside the library? Yes. Where are you? she replied.

Front door of the library. Can I come in?

Be right there.

Megan opened the library's front door with a wide smile, expecting to be met with the same. But when she saw the look on Max's face, her own smile disappeared.

"What's wrong?" she said, opening the door to let the police officer in.

"Let's sit down," Max said.

"No, tell me," Megan said, her heart racing, but she moved without thinking to a cluster of chairs and sat.

Max joined her. "Megan," he said. He looked at her in earnest. "I have to ask you some questions. Officially."

Megan's heart jumped to her throat. "What is going on?" she asked.

"You saw Roman yesterday, is that right?" Max said. "Can you tell me what time?"

Megan shook her head and held out her hands, palms up. "Like, I don't know, three? What's going on, Max?"

"Roman was found dead in his trailer this morning," Max said. "And it looks like you might have been the last person to see him."

"What!" Megan said. She stared at Max without seeing, her jaw open, her mind flashing back to the conversation she'd had with Roman in his trailer. That had only been late afternoon.

How was it possible no one had seen him since then? "Who found him?" she asked.

"The Assistant Director, Heather," Max said. "He was due for a morning meeting and didn't show up and didn't answer his texts, so she went to his trailer. Door was open. Found him inside."

"How did he die?" Megan asked.

Max cleared his throat. "Well, first, why don't I ask a few questions."

Megan paused. She knew what this meant. This wasn't a friendly chat. Officer Max was here to do his job. "Okay," she said.

"Why did you go to see Roman yesterday? Had he invited you over?" Max asked.

"Um, no," Megan said. She wondered briefly if Owen would be arriving soon. The library was due to be opened in an hour. Would she have time to call someone before Max carted her off to—No, she stopped herself. Max had a job to do. That didn't mean he was going to lose all sense of what he knew about her. He would be fair. "I went because of his books," she said calmly. "I wanted to … I mean, if I'm honest I guess I wanted to press him about the strange coincidence. That he'd written books about rock climbing murders, and here we are." And here we are again, she thought.

"Did he welcome you? Did you push your way in?" Max asked.

Megan blinked. Push her way in? "No, of course I didn't push my way in. I knocked. He let me in."

"Was anyone else there?"

"No. Just him and me." She thought back. "There weren't a lot of people around. One crew member who pointed me toward his trailer. There might have been others inside their trailers but mostly it was empty."

"What did you talk about?" Max asked. As she answered, he took notes on his tablet.

Megan strained to remember. "Not a lot. Brenden," she said. "We talked a bit about Brenden. That he was a good climber. I mentioned his ex-wife—Roman's—and how she'd told me about his writing. I told him it seemed like an interesting coincidence. And basically that ended the conversation."

"He was hostile?" Max said.

"Well, not hostile. He was friendly at the start, really. Offered me lemonade and such." She frowned.

"Tell me what else you remember," Max said.

"Well, there was the note I told you about," Megan said. Max nodded. "What else. Well, he was just back from a run. The trailer was pretty tidy, actually."

"Did he get any calls or texts while you were there?"

"No, not that I recall."

"No one else came by?"

"No."

"Did he talk about anyone else he'd seen earlier in the day, or anyone he was supposed to see?"

Megan thought hard. "No, no one. The only thing he said was that someone had ..." Megan stopped.

"Someone had?" Max prodded.

"He said that whenever he went on runs, someone on the crew would leave him a big pitcher of lemonade," Megan said, her mind whirring, connecting dots. She studied Max hard for clues. "How did he die, Max?"

"Can you tell me more about the lemonade? Did he say which crew member left it?" Max said levelly, but Megan could tell just by the tilt of his lips that he was pleased.

"That's it! That's it, isn't it! Something in his lemonade?" Megan said.

Max shook his head. "Megan Montaigne, you are getting ahead of yourself," he said, trying not to laugh. "Did he say who brought the lemonade? Which crew member?"

"He didn't say," Megan said. Her heart suddenly fell. "Max. Max, he offered me some lemonade. I didn't have any, but he offered." She felt a chill.

Max's face fell, as well. "He did? You didn't have any, though?"

"No," she said. "None."

Max blinked hard. "How much did he drink, do you know?"

"He was chugging it," Megan said. "After his run. He just had glass after glass. He'd run eight miles. He was probably feeling pretty dehydrated."

Max nodded and wrote something on his tablet. "Question," he said. "Do you have dry eyes?"

Megan frowned. "Dry eyes?"

"Dry eyes," Max said.

Megan waited for an explanation, or for Max to say he was just kidding. But then she remembered: this was an interrogation, no matter how friendly.

"Well, no?" she said. "Not really?"

"You don't use eye drops of any kind?" Max asked.

Megan shook her head slowly. ".... No?"

"Not for allergies or anything?"

Megan's mind twisted to see where Max was going with this. Something at the back of her mind. Something familiar. Something she'd heard before. "Was there eye drop medication in the lemonade?" she asked. A story she'd read. A poisoning. "Did he die from eye drop poisoning?"

"So I won't find any record of your having bought several bottles of eye drops anywhere?" Max said.

"No," Megan said. "Definitely not. Oh gosh. Max. To think that if I'd been thirsty..." Megan could almost feel the color drain from her face. She felt a little sick. "What a way to go."

"So, then." Max said. "Do you have any theories?"

Megan breathed a heavy sigh of relief. She knew Max had to do his job. But she was glad to feel they were on the same side again. "I don't know. I'll think. That note, the one on the desk that I saw. Did you find it when you went to … to investigate the death?"

Max nodded. "It was there, right where you said it was. 'Meet me at the speed wall tonight. Fox.'"

"Fox!" Megan said. She shook her head. "I knew he was bad news."

"You're getting ahead of yourself there, again, Megan Montaigne," Max said. "All we know is there was a note."

"So one note was from Fox to Roman," Megan said, thinking out loud. "But who was the other letter to? Bee? Was it from Fox to Bee?" Megan laughed. "I sound like I'm reading from a children's book. It almost has to have been sent to Bee, though. Right? Why else was he there that night?"

"All good questions," Max said. "Keep asking. So there's Fox, one person to look into. Who else?"

Megan thought a minute. "Well, Shay," Megan said. "Roman seemed to be harassing her somewhat." Megan bit her lip. She wasn't sure there was much motive there. She raised her eyebrows. "Oh, and Roman's ex-wife, Georgia. Georgia Torkelson. There didn't seem to be much love lost between them."

"Why would she be on set, then?" Max said, also thinking aloud. "Why would he allow her to come by?"

"Marketing," Megan said. "I'm sure, marketing. Gotta use what connections you have. Even if they hated each other, I assume their finances were connected, at least until their kids are grown."

"Anyone else?" Max asked.

"There was that woman yesterday who came by randomly out of nowhere. Bee's ex-girlfriend. Did you talk to her?"

"The station talked to her," Max said. "But I'll be sure to follow up on her, too. Well." Max stood. "Thank you, ma'am, for your time. Please don't leave town. But for now, I think I'm done here."

Megan checked the clock: a quarter to noon. "And just in time, sir, as business is about to open. I'll text you if I hear anything."

"Two and a half hours down, two and a half hours to go," Megan murmured at her computer as the clock ticked past two thirty. She was itching to get out and talk with people. "In the meantime," she said, "as I have a spare minute ..." She opened a browser and typed *eye drops murders* into the search bar.

"Yes," she said as the screen filled with results. "I knew I'd heard of this."

Woman kills husband with eye drops

Man used eye drops to kill his wife for insurance

Woman sentenced for using eye drops to poison husband

"Have people not heard of divorce?" Megan said to the screen. She kept scrolling.

How eye drops can kill

Megan clicked on the last link and started reading. "Tetra ... tetrahydrozoline," Megan said, sounding out the syllables. "Belongs to a family of drugs called imidazoles, which were developed as decongestants and vasoconstrictors. Slows or speeds the heart rate, blood pressure drops dangerously ... blurred vision ... convulsions ... coma ... death." Megan leaned back in her chair. "Eye drops! But how much?" She kept reading, but couldn't find a definitive answer. "But either someone around here was buying a lot of eye drops locally, or they brought them with them," she mumbled.

The library was not terribly busy and Megan looked at the clock impatiently. She texted Owen.

Are you busy? Are you downstairs?

Owen worked in the lower of the level of the library, managing the increasingly busy conference area, as well as the library's social media. He'd recently been getting creative with the library's Instagram, posting photos of books with lego characters acting out key scenes, and had developed quite a following. A reporter from the *Sedro-Woolley Gatherer* had even come out once to talk with him about it.

I'm here, Owen texted back. *Busy but not uninterruptible. What's up?*

Come up and talk with me, Megan wrote.

Is this a Miss Marple thing? Are you solving a murder?

Shut up, Megan wrote, smiling. *Come upstairs.*

Owen didn't answer, but soon his grinning face, topped by his tower of hair, appeared.

"What's up, doc?" he said, leaning against the long desk at which Megan was sitting.

Megan looked around to make sure no one was listening, but the only patrons were a couple of teens in the computer room, a man sitting at a desk next to a stack of books, and a couple of women intensely scanning the backs of books among the stacks, hoping inspiration would lead them to their next favorite read.

"Okay yes, I'm solving a murder. Did you hear?" Megan said quietly.

"Hear what?" Owen asked. He walked around to Megan's side of the desk and pulled up a chair.

"Roman. The producer. He was found dead this morning."

Owen's eyes went wide. "How?" he asked. "Who?"

Megan shook her head. "Your man Officer Max was here just before we opened to ask me questions. I was, it seems, one of the last people to see Roman alive."

Owen snapped. "I always knew you had it in you. How did you do it?"

Megan lightly slapped Owen's arm. "Stop. Max didn't say, but he didn't deny it when I suggested eye drops." She pointed to her computer screen.

"Eye drops?" Owen said, furrowing his eyebrows. "Someone killed him with eye drops?"

"Not in his eyes," Megan said. "Probably in his lemonade. Which, I might add, he offered to me."

"Wow. Did you drink any?"

"Thankfully, no." Megan said. "But this complicates things. Now we're not just looking for who killed Bee, but for who killed Roman. Who would have a motive to kill both of them?"

"All right. So we're brainstorming?" Owen said.

"We're brainstorming," Megan said. "So. It's someone who has access to the film set. Someone who knows how to turn off security cameras." She paused and shook her head. "That part really throws me off."

Owen shrugged. "I mean, it's not that difficult, honestly. I could do it. If I knew where the cameras were and had access. You could even figure it out, I'm guessing."

Megan raised an eyebrow. "Wow, such high praise."

"I'm just saying, don't let that be the wrench in the works. What else do we have?" Owen said.

"Someone who has access to Roman's trailer. Oh and there was a note in Roman's trailer that was a lot like the note I found in the parking lot, only it was signed from Fox."

At this, Owen leaned back in his chair and crossed his arms in front of his chest. "Interesting."

"Interesting?" Megan said. "What are you thinking?"

"Just that there's something about him that I don't like. That doesn't mean he's a killer, though. What would his motive be?" Owen said.

"Good question," Megan said. "There's something I don't like about him, either. Motive, I don't know. Just general arrogance?"

"There would be a heck of a lot more murder in the world if

arrogance were a motive for murder," Owen said.

"Fact," Megan said. She lifted her long dark hair off her shoulder and looked out the window at the bright sunny day. She loved her job, but she would really rather be outside right now, running down leads, talking with Max about ideas and possibilities. "We need to find out more about his relationship with Bee, and with Roman, now, too. I feel like every time I try to talk to Piper, the conversation goes sideways somehow, gets off course. Maybe I can catch her alone tonight. Who else? Have you talked with anyone?"

"Well," said Owen, "interestingly enough I actually have. I saw that other climber, the one who's now the lead …"

"Brenden?" Megan offered.

"Yes, Brenden," Owen said. "I saw him with … I think it's Shay? The one with curly blonde hair." He waved his hand along his head to summon up the image of a cloud of hair.

"Shay Garrick, yes," Megan said. "Tell me more. I'm curious about her, too."

"I saw them out walking together. Something about the way their bodies … I don't know, the way they occupied space, they way they were just closer than normal friends, I just got a vibe that there's something there."

"What were they doing?" Megan asked.

"Nothing, really. But there was a vibe. Like they were canoodling but from a couple feet away from each other. You know? Just that energy," Owen said.

Megan frowned. "I also got the feeling that Shay didn't much care for Roman," she said. "But what does that mean? There are people I don't like, and I don't kill them. Nor do I ask someone to kill them for me."

"Thank goodness," Owen said.

"What does that mean?" Megan laughed.

"It means that if you were task someone with killing someone else, I'm the most likely person you'd turn to, and then I'd have to talk to HR to find out if I had to pay for the murder devices myself, and since we don't have an HR department, it would just get awkward. Plus I'm already busy and we'd need to talk about overtime pay."

"Murder devices?" Megan said.

Owen shrugged.

"Note to self," Megan said. "When hiring out someone to kill someone, do not hire someone who refers to weapons as 'murder devices.'" She shook her head at Owen fondly, then pursed her lips, thinking for a moment. "Hey, question: now that Roman's gone, who's in charge of the movie? How does that work?"

Owen shrugged. "Sounds like a question for google?"

Megan turned her chair back to her computer and typed in the question: *What happens if a producer dies while filming a movie?* She read the screen for a minute. "Wow," she said. "Sounds like everything goes on like nothing ever happened. Kind of sucks for the person who was the victim of the murder devices."

"Who takes over, though?" Owen said, looking over Megan's shoulder to read.

Megan shook her head, still reading. "Subordinate or superior, maybe? Whatever that means. Sounds pretty vague." She leaned back in her chair and looked at Owen. "So we look at who else has some degree of authority. Question: What do you know about Jett?"

ELEVEN

Owen was no help when it came to knowledge about Jett, so Megan spent the rest of the library's open hours trying to decide where she should go to try to find people to talk to. Rae's was always a good choice, as it was a gathering spot. River Rock was bound to have some people milling about. And then there was the hotel the cast and crew were all staying at. Aside from that, anyone who was looking to get away from other people to sort out their thoughts could easily find themselves at one of Megan's personal favorite outside spots, including Addie's Park along the riverfront walk, and the grand cascading waterfalls from which Emerson Falls got its name.

"Too many choices," Megan said as she watched the clock tick closer to five. She tapped her foot impatiently and looked over the library's upcoming program schedule. Book group, a free weekly Italian conversation meetup run by a local who used to live in Italy, a course for seniors in how to use the internet. Everything was running smoothly and the library was gaining visitors all the time, much to her delight.

Four fifty-eight.

Four fifty-nine.

Megan stood and smiled the most compassionate smile she could muster up, trying to look patient as she ushered the last patrons out. With a click she locked the front door, and almost instantly she was racing up the grand staircase to her apartment to grab her purse.

"A stop at Rae's to see who's there, then the hotel," she said to her front door as she locked it behind her. Moments later she was downstairs and in her car for the quick drive to the pub.

Her mind was racing so fast that when she opened the door to the pub she had to remind herself to stop, breathe, and slow down. A look around the room told her she might have better luck at the hotel. She waved at Rae and was about to leave when she noticed a familiar face at a table, alone, looking like she'd decided that "five o'clock somewhere" had started at least an hour or two ago.

Georgia Torkelson.

Even if Roman was Georgia's ex, and even if the relationship had been rocky at best, Megan knew the news of Roman's death would not have been easy to hear. Megan walked over slowly to Georgia's table. Georgia looked up.

"Hey," Megan said softly. "I'm so sorry. How are you doing? Do you need someone to talk to? Or do you want me to leave?"

Georgia looked down into her drink, which at this point was mostly ice. She stared at the ice for a long time, then nodded her head toward the seat across from her.

Megan sat. She sighed. "Georgia, I'm so sorry."

"He wasn't an awful man, you know," Georgia said. She caught Rae's attention and pointed at her empty glass, then held up one finger. Rae nodded. "We weren't great at being married. But as a person, he had some good points." She slurred her words ever so slightly.

"Do you want some … some food? Some fries or something?" Megan asked. Something to absorb the alcohol going into Georgia's system would probably be a good idea.

Georgia shrugged: neither yes nor no. Megan took that as a yes, and quickly went to the counter to order some fries from Rae. She returned with some bread in a basket, as well.

Georgia mindlessly reached for a slice of bread, staring at it without seeing it as she slathered butter on one side.

Megan wondered for a moment who, if anyone, was the beneficiary of Roman's estate. This was not, however, the time to ask.

"Tell me more about him," Megan said. "Tell me about Roman."

Rae came over and silently placed another drink plus a plate of fries on the table. She raised her eyebrows at Megan, winked, and walked away.

"Roman," Georgia said. She picked up a french fry and dipped it in the ranch dip Rae had provided. Georgia shook her head. "This was his absolute dream," she said. "All this. And it killed him."

"This was his dream?" Megan repeated.

"The movie," Georgia said. "He loved climbing but he wasn't that good. He loved the climbers. Idolized them. Wanted to be them. He wrote the books so he could immerse himself in the sport. The kids never wanted to climb and I really think he hated them for it, in a way." She squinted and frowned, took a sip of her drink and licked her lips. "He wanted to raise world class climbers but one of them likes tennis, and the other likes science." She ate a few more fries. "Even though he wasn't very good at climbing, it gave him something. Something that we couldn't. I'm sure that's why he wanted to make this movie. Just to be closer to the climbers. I'll tell you, he wasn't good to his kids, but I guarantee he treated the climbers well."

Megan thought a moment. She remembered Roman saying

that the film, *Inner Ascent*, was somewhat autobiographical. About how climbing had changed his own life. But as far as treating the climbers well, either one of the climbers disagreed, or someone else on the set had an issue with Roman. Alternatively, Megan couldn't dismiss the idea that it could have been Georgia herself, now trying to look like a grieving ex-wife rather than a culprit.

"How did he meet them?" Megan asked. "The climbers, and the people in this movie? Do you know? How he brought this group together? Like Jett, for example. How did Roman meet Jett?"

"Jett," Georgia said, going slightly cross-eyed for a moment and focusing very carefully on getting another fry into the dip. "Jett is a climber, himself, but he's been flimbing climmers … filming climbers for years. Every year there's a climbing festival they all go to. Jett shows his films there. Roman met him at one of those festivals. That's where he met Fox, too. Fox works security on the side. They all have other jobs. Shay is getting a degree in … something … neuro … neuroscience?" The words rolled around in Georgia's mouth. She paused. "Something to do with brains. I think Brenden just climbs."

"Dirtbagger," Megan said, recalling the term.

"Yes, that's right," Georgia said. "Probably that was Roman's dream, too. He loved Brenden. He loved them all." A tear appeared out of nowhere and started to fall down Georgia's face. Others followed quickly as Georgia's nose turned red and she silently cried.

Megan reached for a napkin and handed it to Georgia. "I'm so sorry," she said.

Georgia took the napkin and wiped her eyes and nose gently. "They think I did it, you know," she said.

"They do?" Megan said.

"Always the spouse, you know. That police officer had me

come out to talk to him. Where was I? What was my relationship with Roman like? Was I angry with him about anything?
Of course I was angry with him!" Georgia suddenly realized
she was yelling and people were staring at her. She put a finger
to her lips, shushing herself. "He ignored our kids to be with
these climbers!" she whispered. "But that doesn't mean I'd kill
him! What am I going to do now? How do I tell the kids?" She
started sobbing again, and Megan handed her another round of
napkins.

"Officer Coleman is a fair man," Megan said. "He had to ask
you questions, of course. He's asking anyone who might have
been involved. But he'll do what's right. He always does."

Georgia shook her head. She pushed her drinks and the french
fries to the side of the table, then with her arms as cushions, lay
down her head and cried, silently, tears streaming.

"Is there someone I can call for you?" Megan asked, feeling
quite awkward. She looked over at Rae, who gave her a look
that said "You got yourself into this, you can get yourself out,
sunshine." Megan scowled at Rae, then patted Georgia's arm.

Just as suddenly as Georgia had started crying, she stopped.
She sat up, wiped her tears with napkins, exhaled with determination, and set her resolve. "I'm fine," she said. "I'm always
fine. I'm going for a walk." She looked toward Rae. "Do I pay up
there?" she said, and without waiting for an answer, she wob-
bled and wove her way to the counter.

Once Georgia had left the building, Megan went up to talk to
Rae.

"I hope she's not driving," Megan said. "That's the wife of
the guy who died today. Was killed. Speaking of which, have
your sources told you anything?" Rae was famous for her secret
sources, from which she often gleaned information before anyone else.

"Eye drops," Rae said, "but you probably knew that. Also

there's evidence that Roman had company, if you will, earlier in the day."

"Hmm," Megan said. Her brain flashed to a memory of the rumpled bedspread in the trailer. "Possibly the suspect, possibly not. Anything else?"

"Just that there was initial concern that a local librarian might have been involved, but suspicion has shifted off of her," Rae said with a wink. "That wasn't you who messed up those sheets, was it?"

"Rae!" Megan said, feigning offense. "Of course not!" She shook her head. "But that's a good question. Who was it? I mean for all we know it could have been Georgia. She's been around here a lot, and she certainly gave a good show just now. If it wasn't sincere."

"Seemed sincere," Rae said, shrugging. "People who have had a few rounds have a harder time faking it, in my experience."

Megan nodded. "Speaking of which, I'm going to check that she's not driving somewhere, and then head off to the hotel to see what I can find out. Text me if your sources tell you anything interesting!"

The bright sun blinded Megan momentarily when she walked outside, but soon her vision returned and she could see Georgia in the distance, weaving slightly as she walked, headed away from the parking lot and in the general direction of the riverwalk. Megan breathed a sigh of relief. The last thing they needed was a drunk driver on top of all the current chaos.

Megan had been to the haunted hospital before it became The Grand Skagit Resort and Spa, but she hadn't actually been to the buildings since Sidney Remington had opened the business as a resort. As she rounded the curve to turn into the hotel parking lot, she let out a whistle. "Wow," she said. "Old Sidney did not spare any expense, it seems."

What had once been a wide monstrosity of a decrepit structure now stood as several separate buildings, all gleaming with newness in the sunshine. However, Megan thought that calling the hotel a "resort and spa" might be pushing the envelope of visitor expectations. The hotel was fancier than the chain hotel down the street, but in comparison to resorts in more trendy tourist destinations, this grand resort was quite modest. Clearly Remington was relying on the draw of the hauntings more than anything. A placard next to the lobby entrance gave credence to that idea: a cutout of a ghost rose out of the text proclaiming this to be the "Site of a former haunted hospital. Haunted rooms possible; satisfaction guaranteed!" Below that was information about ghost tours on the grounds and some history of the site. Megan shook her head and went inside.

The front desk was curved into a shape that almost looked like a ghost itself, and was painted a ghostly white. Behind it stood a young woman who smiled at Megan immediately and brightly. Her blonde hair was swept back into a chic bun, and she wore a smooth white shirt with a white blazer without lapels and slim white skirt. On her blazer she wore a pin stylized to look like a very chic ghost. Her perfectly manicured nails were painted in blood red, as were her lips.

"Hi, welcome to The Grand Skagit Resort and Spa! How can I help you today?" she said, teeth shining.

"Well," said Megan, "I'm Megan. I'm hoping you can give me some information. The movie that's filming over in Emerson Falls. Do you have a list of who from the film is staying at your hotel?"

The woman's smile didn't fade. "Are you with the film?" she asked.

"No," said Megan. "Just an innocent bystander. Is it possible to get that list?" She tapped her toes, realizing this might not work out the way she'd hoped.

The woman managed to look both delighted and sad at the

same time. "I'm so sorry, ma'am. I can't give out information about our guests without advance permission. If you talk to the person designated by the film as their official liaison, that person might be able to give you permission and then I'd be more than happy to help." Her eyebrows rose in a combination of sorrow and sincerity.

"Okay, so who would that person be?" Megan said.

"I'm sorry, I can't give out that information," the woman said, smiling.

Megan frowned. "You're not helpful," she said.

"I know, ma'am. I'm so sorry. Guest privacy comes first!" the woman chirped.

Seeing she wouldn't be getting anywhere, Megan turned from the desk. Across from the desk was a small seating area, and there in the seating area, was Shay, watching the whole transaction, looking somewhat dazed.

Megan walked over to her. "Shay, right?"

Shay smiled weakly. "Megan, right? You're friends with Edison. The library lady."

"That's right," Megan said. She sat down. "How are you doing?"

Shay's smile fell. "Honestly, it's all so surreal. It doesn't seem real. What is happening?"

"We're working on it," Megan said.

"You were asking about who is staying here?" Shay said. "I can probably tell you. Almost everyone, basically. Except Fox and Piper, who I think are staying with you?" She looked to Megan for confirmation. Megan nodded. "And Heather. Other than that, I think everyone's here. Group discount." She smiled weakly again.

"It probably doesn't much matter," Megan said, mostly to herself.

"What?" Shay said.

"Oh nothing," Megan said. She chewed on her lip for a moment. "How well do you know all of the people on the film?" she asked finally.

Shay leaned back against the white couch, her curly blonde hair spreading out like a cloud against the back cushion. Megan wondered for a moment how the resort could possibly keep the furniture so clean. Some chemical coating, maybe? She returned her attention to the climber sitting next to her.

"I've known most of them for a while, at least peripherally," Shay said. "Half the crew are climbers, too. Not just the cast. Roman, for example, he's always been around ... was always around." She paused, lost in thought for a moment. "Brenden, Fox, Bee, Piper, obviously they're all climbers. Jett climbs, and he's good, too."

Pleased that the conversation had turned to Jett so quickly, Megan jumped on the opportunity. "I've not had much chance to get to know Jett," Megan said. "Tell me about him. I heard he showed his films at festivals, and that's how he got to know Roman?"

Shay nodded slowly. "I mean, if I'm honest, Roman was sort of a ... almost a groupie. He wasn't a bad climber. Just ... I don't know, overly ingratiating. He wanted so badly to be part of the group. He bent over backward for the climbers. The men, anyway."

Megan caught a whiff of disdain in Shay's voice. "He didn't treat the women the same?"

"Women in climbing are not always treated the same as men in climbing," Shay said. "It's a microcosm of the rest of the world. Men assume your boyfriend taught you to climb or got you into climbing, and even if they're not as good of a climber as you are, they'll offer you beta—that's, like, tips or information about a route—they'll offer you beta while they stare at your boobs or your ass. They'll point you to the easier routes or if you climb something they can't climb they'll say it's because you weigh less or your center of gravity is different. Some guys are stellar, but some guys can't stand to acknowledge the strength of a strong woman, especially if they're not as good as you are."

"Are you a better climber than Roman was?" Megan asked.

Shay laughed. "Definitely," she said.

"Did that bother him?"

"Oh, I think so," Shay said. Her eyes followed along lazily as another hotel guest approached the chic woman at the front desk.

"Did that bother you?" Megan asked.

Shay blinked and returned her attention to Megan. "Roman thought he was pretty important, and he didn't like to be told 'no,'" Shay said.

"You told him no?" Megan said.

"Probably every woman he ever encountered told him 'no' at some point, unless they told him 'yes.' But for sure he asked," Shay said.

"But the guy climbers were all okay with him?" Megan said.

"I mean, they humored him, like I said. Mostly. But when it came to filmmaking, Jett honestly knew so much more. Roman raised the money and wrote the script, and technically he was in charge. But Jett had to stand up to him a few times, I think. Roman had his ideas but Jett has experience and knew what would work and what wouldn't. And Jett's not really the type to give in. They'd worked it out, though." Shay watched the woman talking at the front desk again, and Megan turned her attention to the guest.

"Oh!" Megan said. She realized she recognized the woman. "That's Caitlyn…" She struggled to remember the woman's last name.

"Caitlyn Sheppard," Shay said, an eyebrow slightly raised.

"Do you know her?" Megan asked. "She was … Bee's girlfriend?"

Shay turned to look at Megan and laughed. "Who told you that?" she said.

"Caitlyn did," Megan said. "She wasn't his girlfriend?"

"Only in her mind, maybe," Shay said.

"Did she know him?" Megan asked.

"Oh, she knew him. There are some people, both men and women, who just kind of follow the more popular climbers around. She's one of them. Always going around and standing in front of the climbers and posting selfies with the climbers in the background. She may even have helped him at some point, who knows. Like at a competition or something, helped keep score. It's possible that they went on a date, maybe. But if she thinks she meant anything to any of them ..." Shay shrugged.

Megan nodded, watching Caitlyn at the front desk.

"Jett and Roman did clash a bit," Shay said.

"What?" Megan said, pulling her focus back to Jett.

"Funding," Shay said. "Roman got a lot of funding, but he wanted the actors to get paid well. The climbers. Jett wanted more equipment and crew. But some of it was intended purely for the climbers and that annoyed Jett, that Roman wasted his time on securing funding that Jett thought was unnecessary. I heard them arguing about it once."

"What were they saying?" Megan asked.

"Pretty much that's it. Jett said he needed more funding to make the movie Roman envisioned, and Roman said to just make it work," Shay said.

"Hmmm," Megan said. "Interesting."

Shay stood. "I've got to go," she said, gathering up a floppy bag that had been sitting at her feet.

"Thanks for the chat," Megan said. "Just one more thing. Something keeps bugging me. Everyone assumed Bee was the intended target of the wall sabotage. But the filming was done for the day, and I'm assuming the speed climbing wall would have been prepared for filming in the morning. No one knew anyone was going to be on the wall that night, right? So maybe it would have been set already for the next day's shoot. Maybe Bee was just an unintended victim. Maybe the real target was someone else. Do you know who was meant to be on the wall first thing in the morning? If anyone?"

Shay paused and thought. "Well. Brenden and Fox, I guess. They were meant to film the first scene of the day on that wall." She frowned. "Do you think …?"

"Isn't it possible someone intended for one of them to get hurt instead?" Megan said. "Who would have set the wall?"

Shay tilted her head and the sun through the window touched the edges of her curly hair, giving her a sun halo. "The setters would have set it," she said. "There are a couple of people on the crew who are just setting holds."

Megan mused, mostly just thinking out loud. "Were those people vindictive? Any bad blood there? Or was it someone else? Who went in and cut the rope and took out the set screw? Bee might have just been climbing because he was competitive and obsessed. Maybe someone sabotaged everything thinking Fox and Brenden would be on the wall next, not Bee."

Shay looked unsettled. "I just don't know," she said, considering this new possibility. "You think someone wanted to hurt Brenden? Or Fox?"

Megan nodded slowly. "I don't know, either. But that's interesting. Very interesting." She thought about the notes they'd found. Certainly the notes had been intended to bring people out to climb that night … or had they? Had Bee simply been in the wrong place at the wrong time?

"Anyway, I've got to go," Shay said, looking more and more distressed. "See you later." She pulled out her phone and started texting as she walked away.

"See you later," Megan said to Shay's retreating back.

Megan pulled out her own phone and saw she'd missed a text from Edison.

Reps from Low Gravity Gear flying out tonight to discuss the movie and situation. Filming pushed off another day. Reps eager to head outside to check out the local climbing scene tomorrow morning, 8am, before it gets too warm. Want to come along? I can supply you with equipment (as can LGG).

Megan felt a jolt of excitement. She replied:

Heck yes! Where shall I meet you?

In a moment Edison wrote back:

A bunch of us are going so I'll get a van. Meet at River Rock at 7:30 to gear up. See you then!

Megan then sent a text to Max:

Talked to Shay. Have you looked into the theory that Bee may not have been intended victim?

Max wrote back:

Interesting theory. Can't talk tonight. Will you be around tomorrow?

Megan replied:

Just got a message from Edison about climbing outside tomorrow morning with a gear company that's coming by about the film and funding or something. You should see if you can join! Sounds like many people are going. I'm assuming people involved with the film. Perfect opportunity! Never know what we'll find out!

Several minutes later, Megan got a message back from Max.

I'm in. See you tomorrow morning! Climb on!

TWELVE

A bus and a van were waiting as a small crowd of groggy but excited-looking climbers milled around in the parking lot of River Rock when Megan arrived early in the morning. The sun was climbing up from the horizon in a clear blue sky. Birds chirped enthusiastically, sharing their overnight news. The sound of the nearby river smoothed out the edges of the world. The ground was sparkling with dew and the smell of damp earth filled noses and lungs. The day as new and everything was possible.

But mostly, Megan was glad that so far the day was starting without a murder.

Edison saw her and waved her over to where his staff members Asher, Lexi, and a few other people were standing around with bags of gear and equipment.

"Megan!" Edison said as she approached. "Glad you could come. Let me introduce you to Russ Downs and Natalie Huggins, of Low Gravity Gear. Russ and Natalie, this is Megan Montaigne, our town's Library Director and a great friend."

"And a new climber," Megan said. "So please be gentle with me."

"No problem," Natalie said, and she proceeded to fit Megan with everything she needed for a day of climbing on the ropes: shoes, harness, chalk bag. "We're bringing ropes and the rest of the gear for everyone," Natalie said as she put Megan's harness in a bag for her to carry. "You won't want to put the shoes on until you get to the wall, since they're tight," she said, and she put the shoes and the chalk bag in with the harness.

"Do people ever climb barefoot?" Megan said. As Natalie had commented, the shoes had been quite tight.

"Sometimes," Natalie said. "But not a lot. It's a matter of safety and sanitation. As uncomfortable as the shoes can be, barefoot could hurt a lot more.

Still, Megan was tempted. Maybe that could be her thing. Megan Montaigne, Barefoot Climber.

"Heyyy!" A voice that could have been one of the birds come to life cheerily greeted Megan from behind, and Megan instantly recognized the call of the angels as the voice of Lily Bell.

"Lily!" Megan said, turning to see her friend. Lily was already dressed for climbing, with a bag on her shoulder and a look of enthusiasm on her face. "You're coming along?" Megan said with delight.

"I'm both hired help and eager participant," Lily said. She waved over at where the bus was waiting, pointing to a couple of large coolers. "I brought sustenance. Sandwiches, salads, cookies, snacks, drinks. Edison pays well so I couldn't refuse."

Megan laughed. She, as well as everyone else, knew that Lily would never refuse, regardless of the pay. Lily was one hundred percent reliable, and her sandwiches and cookies were one hundred percent delicious. Realizing she hadn't even thought about bringing any food along, Megan was grateful. Next to the bus and the coolers was a local man named Gary, who worked for the WSDOT but also drove the bus on the side to make some extra cash. Megan waved at Gary. He squinted, recognized her, and waved back with a smile.

"I'm glad you're here," Megan said to Lily. "I know you're not a beginner, but at least you're not a professional like everyone else here. I won't feel so alone!"

"What are you saying about my climbing?" Lily said accusingly, but her eyes sparkled and she laughed. "I'm happy to be here. I've been curious about Ryan's Wall but I don't want to go out there without people who know what they're doing."

"Ryan's Wall?" Megan said. "What's that?"

"It's where we're going today," Lily said. "A climbing area out by Newhalem. Lots of sport climbing, and some bouldering, too."

"Sport climbing?" Megan said, repeating the tone of her previous question. "What's that?"

"Sport climbing. It's where they've permanently bolted the protection—the anchors that you clip your rope into—so you don't have to place gear and don't have to carry a full rack up the wall."

"A rack?" Megan said, raising her eyebrows.

"Uh ..." Lily laughed. "A rack is ... it's a gear harness where you carry your gear, I guess? What you carry with you up a climb. If the anchors aren't already bolted into the wall, you have to carry gear for protection, to catch you if you fall. Otherwise you're just soloing."

Megan didn't ask this time, just raised her eyebrows again.

"Soloing is when you climb without a rope, without a rack, without anything but your shoes, your chalk bag, and your strength and skill," Lily said.

"Sounds like a death wish," Megan said. "Is that what Bee was doing? Soloing?"

"Yes and no," Lily said. "You realize you're asking me a lot of questions and I'm not a professional? I'm not sure what separates bouldering from soloing. Maybe bouldering is a subset of soloing, I guess? But bouldering is generally only for climbs no more than like twenty feet up, maybe thirty. Soloing on big walls is definitely not for beginners." Lily said.

"I think I'll stick to ropes for now," said Megan. "But what about bouldering outside? There aren't any ropes there. What if you fall? Inside the gym the floors are padded. Outside it's … rocks. Ground. Hard ground."

"Crash pads. Like mattresses you carry with you to lay on the ground below you." Lily said. She pointed at the van. "I think the van is mostly carrying crash pads and equipment. Don't worry, they've got you covered!"

A sharp whistle cut through the air and everyone turned to see Edison by the bus, thumb and index finger curled in his mouth.

"I never did learn to whistle like that," Megan said.

Edison waved at everyone to come to the bus, and quickly the group of thirty or so people was on board. Megan sat next to Lily, just behind Edison.

"Wait," said Megan, looking around. "Where's Max? He was going to come, too."

"Driving himself," Edison said, "in case he has to leave suddenly."

"Ah, makes sense," said Megan. She turned and looked again at the gathered crowd. All the main actors were there: Fox and Piper, sitting in separate seats. Brenden and Shay, sharing a seat and talking quietly, smiling. Jett was there, looking like he'd been forced. Megan remembered that Low Gravity Gear was a sponsor and wondered if for Jett, this was a business excursion as much as anything. With everything that had happened the last few days, there was likely a lot to discuss. Going out to climb at Ryan's Wall was the climbing equivalent of doing business on the golf course.

A man was sitting behind Brenden who Megan recognized, but she couldn't place his face. Then it came to her: Troy, Brenden's agent. Was he a climber, too? Megan couldn't remember. But again, it was likely this was a business trip for him as well. Asher and Lexi were there, and a few other climbers and crew members Megan had seen on set.

Megan turned to face forward again, toward Edison. Lily was in a conversation with the person across the bus aisle from them, so Megan focused on Edison.

"So Ryan's Wall," Megan said, leaving the statement open for interpretation.

"Yeah, there's a lot of great climbing opportunities out here," Edison said. "Most of it is undeveloped, though. There was a guy, Ryan Triplett, who did a ton of work on these routes out here. He died while climbing out at Mazama, though. After he died, the climbing community decided to name the wall where we're going after him. 'Ryan's Wall.'"

"Have you been out there before?" Megan asked.

"A few times," Edison said. "Asher and Lexi have gone a lot more than I have. It's great rock. Gneiss."

"It's nice?" Megan said. "A nice place to climb?"

"Gneiss," Edison said. "G-n-e-i-s-s. Metamorphic rock, a lot like granite. Excellent rock for climbing."

"Gneisssssssss," Megan said. "I got it. Is it nice gneiss?"

Edison laughed and nodded. "It's amazing gneiss."

Megan looked back at the climbers. "Is it okay for them to come out?" she asked. "I mean if it's dangerous and all. Do they have something in their contracts that says they can't do anything that could kill them?"

Edison studied Megan for a second. "You're being serious?"

"Yes," she said.

"Well," Edison said. "First, as we've seen, there is also danger off the walls. And second, being on the walls is their job on this movie. Jett has his camera along, and I'm sure will be filming. If he gets good footage it could go in the film. The lines are blurred here. But no, nothing in their contracts."

Megan nodded. The actors/climbers, while maybe slightly more reserved considering everything that had happened, were nonetheless clearly excited to check out a new-to-them rock climbing area. They were talking animatedly amongst themselves, some of them with arms and hands in the air, mimicking reaching for climbing holds on a wall as they talked, likely discussing routes they'd climbed or hoped to climb. She was probably the only one worried here.

Except, she thought, for Troy. Brenden's agent. He looked quite serious, watching the backs of Shay's and Brenden's heads as they whispered. But even he seemed to be dressed for climbing, in a T-shirt and cutoffs that seemed a far cry from the wardrobe Megan had seen him in before. His hair was once again back in a man bun. "Is Troy worried?" Megan asked.

"Brenden's agent?" Edison said. He looked back at the man in question. "Could be. I don't know how much of a climber he is. He's definitely keeping himself inserted in conversations as everything moves forward, making sure he's there as Brenden's advocate anytime we're in film-related discussions."

"We?" Megan asked. "Are you stepping in, then?"

Edison sighed heavily. "Not by choice. But Roman's dead and technically I'm a producer, even if I was meant to be a silent one. Most of the money being put up is mine. Of course there's money from Sidney and the hotel, and from sponsors like Low Gravity Gear and some others. But most of it is from me. And, if I'm honest," he lowered his voice so no one else would hear. "If I'm honest I have a lot more business sense than Jett or Heather or anyone else directly involved with the film. Anyone else who's still alive, that is. I think Roman had a reasonably good head on his shoulders, but … Not to be cruel. It's just a fact. I want this to succeed as much as they do. So I'm trying to help and give advice where I can."

Megan lowered her own voice to match Edison's. "Well, then," she said. "That makes sense. You've been in conversations with them since Roman died?" She tossed her head toward the others in the bus, generally indicating people involved with the film.

"Yeah," Edison said. "Crazy twenty-four hours."

"What's your gut telling you?" Megan said, speaking even more quietly.

Edison shook his head. "You mean who did it? I just can't tell. That's part of why I wanted to gather everyone today. I mean, Low Gravity Gear offered. But I decided to cast a wide net. Invite as many people as would come."

"Get all our suspects together," Megan said. "I knew you were a clever man, Edison Finley Wright."

Edison beamed. "High praise, coming from you," he said. "High praise indeed."

After about half an hour, Gary, the bus driver, pulled the bus off the road. "We're here!" he announced, opening the bus door and then hopping off to unload the equipment stored in the compartments under the bus. The others followed. Asher and Lexi quickly gathered people around themselves to give a rundown of the routes available.

"That over there is Ryan's Wall," Asher said, pointing a bit into the distance. "We're lucky because we're here at the right time of the year. Every year there's a climbing moratorium to protect the nesting habitat of the peregrine falcon. But that season is over and the area is open again. We're near the National Park here, and there have been conflicts over misuse and damage. So if you come back, keep that in mind. We want to protect nature here and work with, not against, the park people."

Lily sidled over to Megan and whispered softly as Asher continued. "Are you ready for this?" she said.

"I don't know," Megan said. "I might watch for a while." She focused on Asher again, who was pointing at the wall and naming routes. An actual rock wall, she realized, was worlds different from a climbing wall in the gym. In the gym, the routes were obvious. Follow the line of yellow holds. Follow the line of orange holds. Follow the line of green holds. A person didn't have to do a whole lot of thinking. But out here, a climber would have to know what they were doing.

"Hey!" Another whisper filled Megan's other ear and she turned to see Max. "You ready?"

"Max!" Megan said, smiling. "I don't know. How do you even know where to climb?" The rock seemed like a mystery.

"If you look carefully," Max said, pointing and squinting, "you can see spots of white on the wall. See? That's chalk. From where other climbers have climbed. That's one way of knowing. Or you can ask other climbers. One thing about climbers, they love to share beta."

Megan had heard the word before, she knew. She thought back. "That's … that's the solution, right?"

"Yeah, basically. It's the information about how to successfully climb a route. Advice, or tips, or things to know about the route like 'there's a really sharp crimpy hold that'll cut you if you grab it wrong.'"

Megan wrinkled her nose. "One: that sounds painful. And two: crimpy?"

"A tiny hold, basically you can only get your fingertips on it," Max said.

"I'm going to need stronger fingers," Megan said, looking at her fingertips.

"And calluses," Max said. "You'll need to build up some calluses. Don't be surprised if your hands start to hurt pretty quickly today."

Asher was finishing up his geography lesson and people were starting to disperse toward the various routes. "Well, I'll give it a try," Megan said. "Which way should we go?"

"There's a 10a route down this way," Max said, pointing off to the east and following his own lead. "One of the easier ones on this wall. Let's start with that."

"I thought a V10 was super hard?" Megan said. "I've only done a V0."

"That's bouldering grades," Max said. "Ropes are graded differently. The grade of 10a actually means 5.10a on the YDS or Yosemite Decimal System. The YDS scale goes from 5.1 to I think 5.15d or something. Compared to a bouldering route, 5.10a is maybe a V0, V1 in bouldering."

"I can do that," Megan said, mostly to convince herself. "Yes, yes I can."

Max and Lily, who both were experienced with lead climbing, climbed up the 10a route to check it out, then came back down to give Megan a lesson in belaying. After a few tries up the start of the route, though, Megan quickly decided she was biting off more than she was ready to chew, and her callus-free hands were already getting sore.

"I think I'll just watch for a while," she said, rubbing her hands together to try to get rid of the pain. Max and Lily nodded and cheerfully got back on the wall.

Megan grabbed a sandwich out of one of the coolers, then looked around for a comfortable boulder to sit on. Seeing the skilled climbers track up the wall like spiders, or monkeys, or mountain goats, made her want to learn more. If they could do that, surely she could learn to, too. It was just a matter of practice and perseverance. Her hands were protesting but her mind was quite intrigued.

Not everyone was on the wall, though. One of the Low Gravity Gear reps, Russ, was talking with Jett and Edison. Megan watched their faces carefully for indications of their moods, and decided they looked amicable. She was relieved. She wanted this to work out, for Edison's sake.

The other rep, Natalie, was talking with Troy, Heather, and Brenden. Megan hadn't seen Heather on the bus, so she assumed Heather must have driven herself up. This group of people seemed more tense. Brenden stood, hands on hips, looking down at his shoes. Troy was gesticulating with his hands as he talked, and the smile he wore seemed forced. Natalie looked like she'd like to get away from whatever discussion was happening there. Heather seemed bored. Megan studied them, but couldn't discern anything further.

She turned her attention to the climbers on the wall. Fox was high on a route, being belayed by someone Megan recognized from the crew but didn't know by name. Piper was belaying Shay. Asher was belaying another minor cast member, and Lexi was doing the same for someone Megan didn't know.

Megan squinted. Wait. She did know that person.

Caitlyn? Definitely. It was definitely Caitlyn.

Megan hadn't seen the woman on the bus. Caitlyn must have found out about the excursion and driven herself. Megan looked over at Max, now taking his turn climbing while Lily belayed him from below. Should she tell him? Would he have his phone on him, to receive a text? She decided it would at least be with Lily, and tapped out a quick message.

As she hit "send," Brenden came and sat with her, a sandwich in his hand. Whatever conversation he'd been having with Troy and the others, Brenden was finished with it.

"So," he said, smiling. "This is your first time on an outside wall?" He looked up at the wall reverently. "Great rock."

"I've been told it's quite … gneiss," Megan said.

Brenden raised an eyebrow and shook his head. "Never gets old."

Megan chuckled at herself. "Have you had a chance to climb yet?"

"Yeah," said Brenden. He looked back over at where his agent was still in conversation with Heather. "Just had to sort through some things."

"All good?" Megan asked.

"It will be," Brenden said. He took a bite of his sandwich. "Mmmm."

Megan nodded. It was clear he wasn't going to say more about his previous conversation, and she decided not to press. "I'm just amazed," she said, pointing to the rock face. "To me these walls look … I mean like rock walls. But you guys seem to see so much more when you look at them. You see things I don't see."

Brenden nodded slowly, chewing, taking another bite, chewing again. "You're a librarian, right?" he said finally.

"Library director, yes," Megan said.

"It's like books. You didn't start out knowing how to read. But you learned. Now, I look at walls, and I know how to read them. They tell me their stories. Reveal their secrets. Show me the way." He paused, looking up at the great rock wall before them as if it were speaking to him right then.

"All that falling, though," Megan said. The padding of the rope walls in the gym wasn't as thick as it was for the bouldering walls, but any kind of padding was welcome in comparison to the rocky ground.

"Falling is how you learn," Brenden said. "There's no glory in it if you never fall."

"It's about glory, then?" Megan asked.

Brenden frowned. "No. That's the wrong word." He thought a while. "Courage maybe. There's no courage in it if you never fall. The whole point of life, the whole work of life, is to build your courage. In everything you do. Climbing is about challenging yourself. Testing your limits and pushing beyond them. It's about making something that seemed impossible, possible."

"Is that what you love about it?" Megan asked. "The challenge?"

Brenden thought a moment. "Climbing teaches you about fear. Some people like to talk about becoming fearless. That's BS. Anyone who believes in fearlessness doesn't know true courage. You can't be courageous if you're not scared. And if you're not scared, you don't need courage. Climbing teaches you how to work through the fear. How to keep practicing until you expand what's within your range of possible. Then you expand it some more. That's how you work through fear. You just keep expanding your comfort zone, one hold at a time. Climbing teaches you that you can do scary things and survive. If that's not applicable to life, I don't know what is."

"But it's dangerous," Megan said. "People die."

"I'm not planning to die," Brenden said. He finished his sandwich in one bite and brushed the crumbs off his hands. "I'm here to fully live," he said. He stood and headed back to the wall.

Megan glanced back to where Brenden had been talking with Troy and the others. Troy and Natalie had left, but Asher was now there talking to Heather. He looked almost flirtatious, even blushing slightly, and Heather seemed … amused, Megan decided. Poor Asher, she thought. Something told Megan that Heather was completely out of his league.

"Okay, then," Megan said out loud, standing. "Fear. Courage." She looked over at the wall where Max and Lily were climbing. Lily was now taking her turn. "I can do scary things and survive. Expanded comfort zone, here I come."

Megan strode over to the wall with her shoulders back, head high, telling herself she wasn't scared. But as she approached the wall, the wall seemed to get taller. She'd seen both Max and Lily struggle and fall. Of course the rope, held firmly by the belay partner, saved them each time. But Megan couldn't help but think of Bee, splayed out on the ground beneath the speed climbing wall.

"Ready to give it a try?" said Max, teeth gleaming, cheeks dimpling. Even the exertion, dust, and sweat in his hair seemed to make him seem more alluring rather than dirty.

"Let's go before I change my mind," Megan said. With the help of her friends, she tied the rope into the prescribed figure eight knot, checked the knot and the harness in the ways she'd been taught in the safety briefing, and started up the wall.

About five holds up, Megan felt her heart beating. She was only a few feet off the ground, but the distance seemed ten times that. She felt herself starting to panic and her hands starting to sweat. As she'd seen the others do a million times, she reached back into her chalk bag, one hand at a time, to dry them off.

"Next hold is your right hand about two feet to your right and a foot up," Max called up to her.

"I can do this," she whispered to herself and the gneiss rock wall. "I can do this." She looked around to see where the rock was dusted with chalk, then reached for the hold, just where Max had said it would be. The hold was good, solid, secure. Megan exhaled. "One hold at a time," she murmured to the wall. She shifted her left foot near to where her right was, then stepped up with her right foot before pushing herself up to stand again. At this point her left hand almost naturally reached for the next hold on the left, and Megan felt a thrill of satisfaction. "I can do this!" she told the wall, but this time with much more confidence. The next hold for her right hand was a bit of a stretch and she shifted several times trying to reach it before finally she caught the hold with her fingertips. She smiled with pride and moved her left foot …

… And then she slipped. Her right hand flew off the wall and both feet fell off their holds as her heart leaped to her throat. For a moment Megan held on with her left hand but she lost that grip, too. All within a fraction of a second, the feet, the hands, and in a moment she was free-falling for what seemed like forever though in reality it must have been milliseconds, and then …

Megan felt a jolt as Max caught the slack of the rope, holding tight to the rope to keep it secure within the belay device.

"I got you," Max called up. "I got you."

Megan felt time swirling around her. So much had happened in that moment she was falling. She could have composed a symphony in how long it took her to fall. Written a novel. Gone to college. The fall had expanded time, and now as she sat dangling in her harness next to the wall, all of time was snapping back to the present.

"I'm okay," Megan said in a voice so weak she wasn't sure Max would have heard. She breathed hard. She willed her heart to slow back to normal, willed the sandwich she'd eaten not to make a reappearance.

And then she smiled.

"Lower me down?" Megan called down, and Max did. When her feet touched the dirt she struggled to land elegantly but ended up on the ground.

"You did great," Max said, his grin wide and encouraging. "Everyone falls."

"That's what Brenden was telling me," Megan said. She looked up at the wall, trying to figure out where she'd fallen from. She was amazed at how high she'd gotten, really. Taller than Max, certainly. Taller than a one story building. Maybe even two.

"Want to go again?" Max said enthusiastically.

Megan looked at her hands. She hadn't realized it, hadn't even felt it, but at some point along the way she'd cut her finger and it was bleeding. She looked at Max. "Yes," she said. "Definitely. But not right now. But put it in your calendar as a rain check. It's a date."

Asher had brought over the first aid kit and had helped sanitize and wrap Megan's finger. She stared at the bandage as if it were a badge of honor.

"I suppose you're not really a climber if you haven't had an injury?" Megan said, smiling up at Asher from the boulder she was sitting on.

"Definitely," Asher said. "The first of many, if you keep it up."

"I think I just might," Megan said. "I fell, and I survived." She glanced over at where Max and Lily were still climbing, on another route. "11a," Megan said to herself, rolling the climbing lingo over on her tongue. The route she'd been climbing was graded 5.10a, and the one her friends were on now was graded 5.11a. "11a," she repeated. Max and Lily were laughing even as they fell. Both of them, she realized, were brave. Courageous. Maybe that was part of what she loved about them. They weren't afraid to try, and they weren't afraid to fall, literally. Her thoughts felt warm and her heart was almost literally bursting. Good people. Good friends. People who inspired her to be better, too.

"Asher," a woman's voice said, accompanied by the sound of feet on gravel. Megan turned and saw Heather approaching.

"Not climbing today?" Megan said. It was obvious Heather was not climbing, if only by the way she was dressed. Her sleek black pants had spots of chalk at the hem and the thigh, and her black boots were nearly covered in dust. Her black sleeveless turtleneck was attractive but hardly appropriate for climbing. The black handbag she carried was almost a satchel, and undoubtedly carried work in its depths.

Heather didn't answer, but merely blinked slowly, as if annoyed by a mosquito that she really wasn't going to worry herself about.

"Asher," Heather said, reaching into her bag. "I have a list of equipment we need for the shoot, whenever we get around to shooting again." Her annoyance did not stop with Megan, apparently, Megan thought.

Heather fished around in her purse until she found what she wanted. She handed a piece of paper to Asher. "Can you gather these for us? Edison said it would be all right."

Asher gazed at Heather with a look that intrigued Megan. Did he have a crush? Megan had seen Asher talking with Heather before, and hadn't he been blushing then? Megan smiled inwardly, wondering what the situation was. Heather was a striking woman, if emotionally sharp. And Asher was sweet, and handsome in his own ragged, near-dirtbag way. Megan smiled again at her mental use of the climbing jargon "dirtbag."

"No problem, Heather," Asher said, but Heather had already turned and walked away.

"That's nice of you," Megan said to Asher. "Very helpful." She tried not to look amused.

"Ah, that's what we're here for," Asher said, watching Heather walk away. "Edison told us to help them with whatever they need, so." He looked down at the list and started reading it.

Megan's eyes followed his, and then widened.

"Asher, can I … can I see that note real quick?"

Asher shrugged and handed the note to Megan.

But it wasn't the note Megan was interested in. It was the paper.

The exact same paper as the note she'd found in the parking lot.

The exact same paper as the note she'd seen in Roman's trailer.

THIRTEEN

Stepping carefully through the scattered rocks on the ground, Megan raced over to the wall where Max was just lowering Lily down from a climb. "Max!" she said breathlessly. "Paper! Heather has paper like the notes Roman got, and the one in the parking lot!"

Max shifted his head slightly toward Megan without taking his eyes off Lily. "What?" he said.

"Heather," Megan said. "Heather gave Asher a note. I swear it's the exact same paper as what we found." Megan knew that keeping Lily safe was more important in this very moment but she wished Max would hurry up.

Finally, Lily was on the ground and Max turned his attention to Megan.

"Okay, now I can listen. When was this?" Max asked.

"Just now," Megan said. She pointed toward where she'd been sitting. "I was over there, and Asher was bandaging my finger. Heather came by and gave him a note."

The sun was high in the sky, beaming down against the rocks, which reflected its heat and light. Max squinted into the glare. "Where is she now?" he asked, eyes scanning the climbing area.

Megan looked around as well. Where had Heather gone? She'd be almost impossible to miss in her all-black outfit amongst this group of chalky cutoff sweatpants and raggedy tank tops, of dirty cargo pants and T-shirts emblazoned with the logos of climbing gear companies.

"Was she on the bus?" said Lily, who had joined the search.

Megan sighed. She'd just spotted Heather getting into a small red car. "No," she said, pointing. "Apparently not. She's leaving."

Max nodded, undeterred. "Okay. Start from the beginning." He looked around once more. "Asher's still here. Tell me what you know and then we'll talk to him. But Megan," he said. "Remember that paper is paper. Unless Heather made it herself, it's likely other people have similar paper."

"I realize that, detective," Megan said, a twinge of sarcasm slipping into her tone. "There's not much more to tell."

"Did she write on the paper in front of you? Do you know that it was her writing? Or had someone given her the note to pass on?" Max asked.

Megan frowned. "Well, no, and no, and I don't know." She heaved a sigh of frustration.

"Come on," Max said. "Let's talk to Asher."

They found Asher at the wall. They had to wait a few minutes until Asher had lowered a crew member he was belaying, but then Max pulled Asher aside.

"Asher, we have some questions for you," Max said quietly. "Do you have a minute?"

Asher went slightly pale in realizing Max's mission was official. "What did I do?"

Max laughed. "I don't know; did you do something we need to know about?"

Asher's color didn't return. His eyes remained wide. He didn't know Max well and had no clue the officer was joking with him.

Max cleared his throat. "Anyway," he said. "Megan says Heather gave you a note a few minutes ago."

Asher looked from Max to Megan and back. "Yeah?" His brow furrowed in confusion. "Was that not okay? Edison told us to—"

Max shook his head. "No, it's fine. We just are curious about the note. Do you still have it?"

Asher reached into his back pocket and pulled out the slightly crumpled note. He handed it to Max.

Max looked at the note, then at Megan. He gave her a small nod. He turned back to Asher. "Do you have your phone on you? Any chance you could take a picture of the information on the note and let us keep this?"

Asher's brow furrowed further. "Uh … I guess? But … I mean it's just a list of equipment. Is there anything wrong on there?"

Megan spoke up. "Asher, how long have you known Heather? Did you just meet her with the film shoot?

All of Asher's color now returned to his face, and then some. Either he'd been out in the sun too long, or he was blushing again. "Well," he stammered. "I mean we met just with this film shoot."

Megan glanced at Max. She could tell his interest was piqued at this line of questioning, and at Asher's reaction. The corner of Max's lip turned up and he nodded once at Megan, indicating that she should continue.

"It seems like you know each other pretty well already, though?" Megan said.

Asher's color went even deeper red. "I mean, she's an attractive woman," he said.

"What does that mean?" Megan said. "Have you and she … you know?"

"Have we what!" Asher protested almost immediately.

"Nothing?" Megan asked.

Asher quickly looked back and forth between Max and Megan. "What?" he said. "Is it illegal? We hardly did anything. And she started it."

"Started what?" Megan asked.

Asher looked at Max, hoping perhaps for Max to put an end to this line of questioning. Max merely raised his eyebrows expectantly.

"She came onto me," Asher said. "The first day. Before everyone else was here. She came onto me. I mean, who am I to refuse when a pretty woman wants ... I mean, it's not illegal. Why are you asking all of this?"

"Can you just tell us what happened when Heather seduced you?" Megan said. "I don't mean all the details. Just the broad strokes."

Max's lip quivered momentarily and then he resumed a professional face.

Asher looked at the wall as if hoping it would save him. He shook his head. "She just ... starting coming onto me. Seducing me, like you said. Asked if there was somewhere private we could go."

"And was there?" Megan asked.

Asher shrugged. "I guess."

"Where did you go?" Megan asked.

"The office, okay? We went back into the office. The back part of Edison's office," Asher said.

Megan nodded. She looked at Max. "No further questions, your honor."

Max gave a small laugh. "That's it from me, too. Thanks, Asher."

Asher shook his head again and headed off to vent his embarrassment and frustration on the rock wall.

Max turned to Megan. "So, are you going to tell me? What was all that about?"

"Do you know what's in the back part of Edison's office?" Megan said, smiling.

Max's smile grew as he realized what Megan had figured out.

"The security camera system. The backend of the security system," Max said.

"Exactly what a person would need to know, if, for example, they wanted to turn off the security cameras," Megan said.

Max beamed at Megan, his smile as bright as the sun burning overhead. "I knew there was a reason I keep you around," he said.

"Yes," Megan said. "You're a smart man. But the question is: what next?"

"I'll ask Heather about the paper," Max said. "But don't get your hopes up. Like I said, it could be sold anywhere. If she bought the paper at a local store, then probably half the people in Emerson Falls have some like it."

Megan frowned. "I suppose it would be a bit much for everyone to always give me a list of everything they buy," she said.

"Maybe a hair over the top," Max laughed.

Megan put her hands on her hips to help her think. What next, indeed?

As she thought, she absently gazed on the scene of climbers before her. Until suddenly her eyes came into focus on one woman: Caitlyn.

"That woman over there," Megan said, pointing subtlety. "Caitlyn Sheppard. Did you talk with her?"

"Only briefly," Max said. "I saw her at Rae's and asked her a few questions but she was on her way out and I didn't really have reason to keep her."

A tickle of sweat dripped down Megan's neck. The sun was warm and the walls reflected the heat and blocked the breeze. Aside from the sound of an occasional car whipping by on Highway 20, or the grunts and yells of the climbers and the calls of encouragement from their partners on the ground, it was silent. The air carried little wind but held the weight of the climbers' efforts, a sort of anticipatory tension.

"My turn to ask the questions, then," Megan said.

Caitlyn was not climbing but rather had perched herself on a rock near where Fox and Brenden were now scaling the wall. Her long blonde hair was plaited into two girlish braids, and she was subconsciously—or flirtatiously, but no one was looking—playing with the end of one braid now. Megan noticed with surprise that Caitlyn was adorned with carefully applied makeup, and her fingernails were painted a bright candy pink. Her top was a neon pink workout bra with straps in back almost as intricately braided as her hair, and her black workout tights had open lattice down each side. As Megan approached, Caitlyn was positioning herself in her camera frame with Brenden and Fox in the background. She turned her head, lifted her chin, pouted her lips, dipped her eyes, all trying to find the perfect position for a casual, unposed selfie.

"Hey," Megan said.

Caitlyn looked up, startled. She grinned. Megan almost flinched at how shallow Caitlyn's smile seemed.

"Hi," Caitlyn said. "I know we've met but I'm sorry …"

"Megan," Megan said. "Megan Montaigne. You're a climber?"

"Yeah, sort of," Caitlyn giggled.

"You seem to know these guys," Megan said, nodding toward Fox and Brenden. "Are you friends?"

"Yeah," Caitlyn said, pleased. "Totally."

"You mentioned that you were Bee's girlfriend," Megan said. "How are you doing?"

As if remembering she was meant to be mourning, Caitlyn's smile faded immediately. "Oh it's hard, you know," she said. "I can't believe he's gone." Her lips quivered.

Megan could feel the insincerity oozing off Caitlyn, but nonetheless she stood silent a moment to let Caitlyn grieve. After a bit, Caitlyn let out a shuddering sigh.

"It's so hard," Megan said, watching the young woman carefully.

"I just ... I don't know," Caitlyn said.

"Did you know Roman, too?" Megan asked.

Caitlyn's eyes darted immediately to Megan's. She paused. "I mean everyone knows everyone," she said. "It's a tight-knit community."

A vision of the rumpled bed in Roman's trailer suddenly flashed through Megan's mind. "Did you happen to see him on the day he died?" she asked.

Caitlyn was silent again for a few moments. She seemed to be trying to assess the correct answer. Which gave Megan the answer she needed, but she waited for Caitlyn to speak, nonetheless.

"In the morning?" Caitlyn said.

"You saw him in the morning?" Megan said.

Caitlyn nodded.

"Were you at his trailer?" Megan asked. Caitlyn didn't answer right away. "I'm not judging, Caitlyn. I'm just trying to figure things out."

"I just think I might like to go into the movies one day," Caitlyn said. "People tell me I'm a great actress. I thought it would be good to get to know him. He was a nice guy." Her eyes got watery and Megan felt this time she was sincere.

"What can you tell me about when you saw him?" Megan said. She paused. "Were you ... intimate?"

Caitlyn lifted one shoulder and looked away. *Yes, what's it to you?*

"Did anyone else come by when you were there?" Megan asked.

"Not when I was there," Caitlyn said. "I left when he went out for a run."

"Did you leave before him or after?" Megan asked.

"I guess at the same time?" Caitlyn said, the upturn of her voice turning the statement into a question.

"Who was the last out the door?" Megan said. "What I'm getting at is, did whoever leave last lock up?"

Caitlyn's face shifted into pain. "I mean I guess I left last? I don't have a key, do I, so I couldn't lock up?"

"Did you see anyone else around?" Megan said. "Cast or crew or … anyone?"

"Well, his ex-wife," Caitlyn said. "Roman's ex-wife. She came by while we were … talking."

Megan blinked. This was an interesting development. "Did you see her?" she asked.

"She yelled through the door, which is next to the bedroom," Caitlyn said.

Megan remembered the trailer's layout and in her mind confirmed that this was true. "What did she say?"

"Something about child support," Caitlyn said. "She was mad that he was ignoring the kids."

"Did she come in to talk to him?" Megan asked.

"No," Caitlyn said. "We pretended not to be there." She shrugged.

"And she was gone when you left?"

"Long gone."

Megan took this in. "Tell me about Heather," she said. "Heather Birdsong. The Assistant Director. Do you know her?"

Caitlyn looked over toward Fox. "No, not really," she said. "I met her earlier. You sort of want to not like her but I think there's more to her," she said.

Megan thought back to Edison's comments about Heather. The woman was a dilemma, Megan thought. A conundrum. A conundrum with familiar paper.

"And Fox?" Megan said. "Brenden?" She paused. "Piper?"

Caitlyn shrugged again. "They're fine. They've been planning Bee's funeral," she said. "He's—he wasn't really close to his family. The climbers are going to take his ashes to El Cap. They're going to climb up the Nose and scatter the ashes from the top."

"El Cap? The Nose?" Megan said, raising her eyebrows.

"El Capitan," Caitlyn said. "It's in Yosemite. It's a … I mean it's a big wall. A big rock. A big rock wall. Where tons of people climb. The Nose is one of the routes up to the top." She looked at the wall where the people in question were climbing, focused. Not paying any attention to her. She frowned. "I mean is it so much to ask that they take me seriously?" she said. "I'm not the world's best climber, but they think I'm a joke and they think I don't know. There's no reason for that. It's just mean. They think they're so special. Movie stars. I hang around because …" She trailed off, staring at the climbers, lost in thought. "Roman understood," she finally said. "He really loved them. He watched out for them. He really wanted to be one of them. And now …" Caitlyn's smile was completely gone. She suddenly stood, grabbed a T-shirt she'd discarded onto the rock next to her, and left.

Megan watched as Caitlyn walked away, visibly upset. Caitlyn passed by Troy, who stopped her and said something to her. Caitlyn waved her hand dismissively, but Troy said something else, and then he started walking with her toward where a few cars were parked. Caitlyn handed something to Troy—Megan thought maybe car keys—and Troy got into the driver's seat. Caitlyn got into the passenger side of the car, put her hands on her face, and sobbed.

"Well," Megan said to the back of the car as it drove away. "At least she's not driving, I guess."

Megan saw Edison approaching her, looking content, peaceful. Like he was in his element. She couldn't help but return his smile.

"Everything okay?" Edison said, clapping his hands to remove some of the chalk dust but not realizing there was a stripe of dust on his forehead. "I saw you in deep conversation with a bunch of people. Can I assume Megan Montaigne is on the case?"

"Megan Montaigne is on the case!" Megan said. "Having fun?"

"There's nothing better than getting out here with people who are so much better than I am," Edison said, looking back toward the climbers still on the wall. "I learn just by watching them. And they're so generous in offering help and tips."

"Beta," Megan said, proud of herself for remembering the lingo.

Edison's eyes crinkled. "Beta, yes, and also climbing techniques, tips on how to move more efficiently or reach farther." As he spoke, he was rubbing his forearms. "I'll feel this tomorrow, but it's been a great day."

"We definitely should come out here again," Megan said. "Once all these film people are gone. Although I suppose they have to make a stop at … El Cap?"

"Ah, El Capitan," said Edison. "Yeah, to spread Bee's ashes. The Low Gravity Gear people have offered to pay cremation expenses. They've been incredible through this whole thing. I don't think the film could have happened without them. But they really are excited about helping new people discover climbing, and supporting the climbers we have here. They're great partners."

"I saw you talking with that Russ guy, and with Jett," Megan said. "Are you pretty much in charge now?"

Edison put his hands on his hips and a shadow of seriousness fell over his face. "Yeah, I guess. I mean Jett will really give the day-to-day guidance now, along with Heather."

"They're not going to put the movie on hold?" Megan asked.

"Seems with two deaths there would be good reason. And legal reason."

Edison shook his head. "I hear where you're coming from. I offered the idea to Jett, told him it would be fine with me if he wanted to wait until he had someone to replace Roman. But Jett didn't seem to think that was necessary. The cost of sending everyone home and then bringing them back to set again, organizing all the locations, all of it, he said it would double the budget. I don't know if that's exactly true, but ..." He shrugged. "Anyway, we're working on it. Max is having someone at the station find and make copies of the relevant files and emails on Roman's laptop for me, and then we'll just go from there."

"You're grace under pressure, Edison Finley Wright," Megan smiled. Then she remembered her conversation with Asher. "Say, Edison Finley Wright," she said.

"I can't tell if I'm in trouble when you use my full name?" Edison laughed.

"No!" Megan said. "No, mostly I just like the sound of your full name. But I'm wondering about Asher."

Edison scanned the gathered crowd for sight of his employee. "What about Asher?" he said. "Is he in trouble? Do you need his full given name?"

"Well, I don't know about trouble. But I have reason to suspect he may have let Heather into your office, where the security camera system is, to make out with Heather."

Edison's eyes popped wide. "With Heather? What makes you think that?"

"He basically told us that. Max and me."

Edison sighed. "I mean I suppose technically it's not against company policy, but it does go a bit against the standards I'd like to see in my business." He frowned.

"Well, I'm less concerned about standards than I am about the security camera part. What I'm wondering now is whether

Heather could have accessed the system to turn it off, at the end of the shooting day."

Edison grimaced. "It was all pretty chaotic. Organized chaos, but there was so much going on, and no one thought anyone was going to be any monkey business. It's possible, I guess."

Megan smiled to herself at Edison's use of "monkey business."

"Is there any way to find out who was in your office?" Megan said. "Did they take fingerprints or anything?"

"Even if they did, Heather was in there with me at least a couple of times."

"The day Bee died? Did she come in at your request or did she come on her own?"

"Hmmm. I can't remember. What are you getting at?" Edison asked.

"I'm just wondering if she'd already made out with Asher, had scoped out the system, and was working on spreading around her DNA and fingerprints while you were in the room so she'd have an alibi. Did she comment on the security system? Did she touch it?"

Edison thought for a moment, then groaned. "She might have. She went over to that desk and sort of cleared things aside to lean on it while she was talking to me. But Megan, I've told you. There's something about Heather that reminds me of myself. I just don't think she's the type."

"The murdering type?" Megan said.

"Yeah, if we're being blunt. Yeah."

"People thought the same thing about Ted Bundy," Megan said.

"What is it with people's fascination with Ted Bundy?" Edison said. "It's, what, forty years later now and people still are obsessed with him."

"I think it's exactly that," Megan said. "That people didn't clue into the fact that he was, in fact, the murdering type. The people around him were clueless about him. Ann Rule starting writing her book *The Stranger Beside Me* about a serial killer before she had any idea that the person she was writing about was the same guy she worked volunteer shifts with—alone—at the crisis clinic. Bundy's own girlfriend didn't think he was a killer. Women he picked up to murder went along willingly. I think we want to know more about him because we want to know: Would I have known? How are my instincts? What did those other people miss and would I have seen it? I really think it's not morbid fascination, but rather survival instinct. We want to know what other people missed, so that maybe we would know better if the same thing happened to us."

Edison shrugged. "Could be, I guess. At any rate, don't jump to conclusions about Heather. Okay? Just be careful."

Megan nodded. But as far as fascination went, she was fascinated that both Asher and now Edison had fallen for her charms. And Fox, too, she remembered. There was just something about Heather, apparently. Whether Megan could see it herself or not.

"I'm getting back on the wall," Edison said. "While I have these experts here. You coming?"

Megan held up her sore hands. "I think I have to wait until I've built up the calluses. Besides, I need to get home and get showered for work. I'm hoping Max is ready to go and can drive me. Be careful up there! We need you in Emerson Falls!"

With a wave, Edison ran off. Megan hadn't lied. She did need to get home and get showered for work, but she still had plenty of time. But now she had a new mission: finding out about Heather.

FOURTEEN

Max dropped Megan off at the library—her home—and quickly she was showered, dressed, and down on the main floor, opening up the library for the day. Megan greeted the patrons who were at the door waiting, and felt the rush of fresh warm air from outside.

"An outdoor library," Megan said. "Has anyone thought of that? An outdoor library." Her lungs felt healthier just by virtue of her time spent out by the rock wall at Newhalem, climbing up the rock and basically hugging nature with her whole body. She loved her library, but she also loved how alive she felt outside. Before heading to her desk, she went to the windows on the river side of the library and flung them open.

"I suppose the books wouldn't weather well in an outside library," Megan said, but she wasn't quite ready to dispose of the idea. Humans were part of nature, but too often, she knew, humans were apart from nature.

When she sat down at her computer, the first thing Megan did was research climbing shoes.

"Seems I'm hooked," she said to herself, pleased.

A quick look at all the options, however, let Megan know she needed more advice before diving in. "What, exactly, is an 'aggressive' shoe?" Megan wondered out loud, her eyebrows furrowed. "Is that a shoe with an attitude?" She saw that there was a shoe named after and designed with the help of Tommy Caldwell, whose autobiography she'd shelved earlier. She was almost tempted to impulse buy those shoes, until she saw the price. Apparently being one of the best climbers in the world meant that the shoes named after you were not cheap.

"Okay, then," Megan said, turning her attention to Heather. She typed into the search bar.

Heather …

What was Heather's last name? Megan stared into space, trying to recall. Something unusual. Something that hadn't seemed to fit …

Heather Assistant Director

Megan hit "submit" but didn't feel much hope that such a vague search would bring up what she wanted. What she really needed was a search engine for her brain.

She was correct in her assumption. The search brought back thirty-one million results, and on the first page, not one Heather's name was repeated.

"A heck of a lot of Heathers with long blonde hair," Megan mused as she flipped through the pictures. Finally one stood out: a petite, angular woman with short, angular nearly black hair and dark, angular glasses. "Birdsong!" Megan read. "Of course!"

From outside the window, a bird trilled its musical call.

"You could have told me that earlier," Megan said to the bird.

Heather Birdsong, Megan typed into the search bar, and then she scanned the results. It seemed Heather had been on the arm of dozens of different men over the years. Megan wondered: did she just not want to settle? Or was she too difficult to stay with? Even on this movie alone Heather had already been with Fox, had seduced Asher, and perhaps had her eye on Edison.

"She'd better not," Megan muttered under her breath.

Megan clicked through to the news stories. She didn't find much, but there was one old article in which a small-town paper had interviewed Heather, at the time new to Hollywood, about her career path.

Heather knew the path to success would be rough. But Heather was used to rough. Family troubles meant Heather left home at the ripe age of fifteen to move in with a young aunt. She quit school and took on any job she could find: waitressing, working at the local record store, barista at a coffee shop, cleaning houses when she could find the work. At the record store she met a few members of a band called Colloidal Blue. On seeing her organizational skills, the band coaxed her into helping them film a music video.

"I wasn't paid for it," says Heather. "But I was curious. I wanted to see what it entailed. I knew I could do it. I never doubted it. I just wanted to see what it was like."

As it turned out, Heather was hooked. When she was eighteen she moved to Los Angeles. There, she got a job as a personal assistant to film mogul Hal Mookum, who took her under his wing. She was undisturbed by rumors of an affair between the two of them.

"Hollywood is all about rumors," she says. "If you have a thin skin, you need to get out. I did what I needed to do to get where I want to go. It's that simple. If men do it, people expect it. If women do it, people look down on us. That's their problem, not mine."

Megan scanned the rest of the article but found nothing more of interest. Heather had a point, she thought. A man acting the way a Heather apparently had wouldn't raise a single eyebrow. But a bold, strong woman was too much.

But still, that paper.

She clicked back into the search bar to do a quick search on Bee. But she couldn't remember his name.

Bee climber

Nothing.

Bee rock climber in film Inner Ascent

Megan smiled to herself when that search yielded results. "Enzo Larrabee. You don't get to be Library Director without some gnarly search skills," she said to the screen. She scanned through a few articles on Bee and found that he, too, had had a rough childhood. Father died when he was ten. Mother was controlling. He left home at eighteen. Mother tried to finagle her way back into his life when he started being successful in climbing and a few films. A friend of his saw his success and wanted that same success, so started climbing as well. Big fight between Bee and the friend when the friend couldn't reach the same level of success on his own.

"Success comes from following your own passion, not someone else's," Bee said.

Megan pondered a moment. Was that friend a suspect?

She thought again of the cremation and memorial the other climbers had planned for Bee. Would his mother and friend want to be there? Or would they have lost interest in Bee, now that he could do them no more good? Now that they could no longer try to use him?

"Hey, Boss!"

Megan looked up to see Owen walking toward her desk. She tilted her head to get a better look at him. Had he gotten a haircut?

"Did you get a haircut?" she said.

Owen ran a hand through his tall flop of hair. "Yeah, this morning. I was starting to look like an unshorn sheep."

Megan laughed. "What's up? All good downstairs in conference and convention world?"

"All good. What's up here?"

"Research," Megan said, leaning back in her chair. "Say, have you thought about your funeral? What you want?"

Owen threw his head back and laughed. "Is this your way of telling me you're going to kill me?"

Megan smiled. "No, of course not. I need you too much! Bee's friends are going to cremate him and toss him off a rock wall in Yosemite National Park."

"Seems fitting," Owen said. "No, I haven't thought about it. Have you? Is there anything I need to know?"

"Well, hopefully I don't need it for a long time, either. But yeah, I've heard you can now be composted. Literally just return to the earth."

"That's different from being cremated and potted in with a tree?" Owen said.

"Yup. You're in a big heap of compost and you decompose and other people are composted on top of you."

Owen shuddered involuntarily. "And then Sidney Remington comes along and makes the compost heap into a haunted hotel," he said.

This time it was Megan who laughed. "Probably true," she said. She thought another moment. "I'm baffled, Owen," she said. "Bee, then Roman. Earlier it occurred to me that Bee's death could have been intended for someone else. The wall may have been set for the film shoot the next day. The first scene that was going to be shot that morning was Fox and Brenden on the speed climbing wall. Maybe the sabotage was intended for one of them?"

"Who would know?" Owen said. "Who would know more about who set the wall and the schedule?"

"Well, Roman," Megan said. "But also Heather."

"Sounds like you need to talk to Heather," Owen said.

"I really need to talk to Heather." She looked at the clock.

"I see that look on your face," Owen said, smiling. "I've got everything under control here if you want to get out."

"I don't even know where Heather is staying," Megan said. "She's not at the hotel."

Owen raised an eyebrow, already reading Megan's mind. "Good thing you know someone with connections to all the local hospitality," he said.

"Good thing," Megan said, casting Owen a conspiratorial smile. She pulled out her phone and read aloud as she tapped out a message to Lily:

Do you know where Heather Birdsong, Assistant Director on the film, is staying? She's not at the resort.

Megan looked at Owen and nodded. "Good to have friends in a lot of high places," she said.

They waited a minute before Lily texted back:

I don't, but I'll send out the bat signal and find out. Will let you know ASAP. Super busy today, might take a while. Sorry!

No worries, Megan replied.

"Liar," Owen said, smiling. "If she gets back to you soon and you want to leave, just let me know. I'm downstairs." He headed back to his office.

Unfortunately Lily didn't get back to Megan in time for her to take Owen up on her offer. By the time Lily replied, it was nearly five o'clock: closing time.

Sorry I took so long, Lily wrote. *Not as easy as I thought it was going to be! She's renting a vacation home. Let me copy the address for you …*

Megan looked at the address and didn't recognize it right away, but luckily the internet knew exactly where it was. Slightly out of town, on the river, past where Edison lived. Megan sent the directions to her phone, then shut down her computer. She picked up her phone and dialed Owen's extension.

"Emerson Falls Library conference serv—oh, it's you," Owen said. "Hey. What's up?"

"Finally heard back from Lily. I'm heading out to Heather's. She's at a vacation home just east of town. I'm going there now. In case I don't return and someone needs to know where to find my bloody body."

"That's a bit morbid," Owen said, "but a good plan. We should probably microchip you, come to think of it."

"That's just asking for someone to come along and cut the microchip out of me," Megan said.

"Again, a bit morbid."

"Same reason I don't use my fingerprint to open my phone," Megan said.

"Because someone would … cut your finger off and steal your phone?" Owen said, incredulous amusement in his voice.

"Exactly," said Megan. "And same reason I don't use facial recognition."

"Because someone would steal your phone, cut off your head, and carry it around with them everywhere in a bowling ball bag, just so they could use your phone," Owen said. His tone had turned toward mockery.

"It could happen," Megan said.

"I suppose anything's possible," Owen said. "Always thinking, you are."

Megan could almost picture him tapping his brain with his fingertip. "You laugh, but just you wait, one day we'll hear about people whose heads were cut off so people could access everything tied to their facial recognition software. Who will be laughing then?"

"Not the people whose heads were cut off," Owen said. "Because they'll be headless, you see."

"You're a quick learner, Owen Scott," Megan said. "That's why I hired you. You can thank me later. Anyway, I'll text you when

I'm back."

"Sounds like a plan," Owen said.

Ten minutes later Megan was in her car, windows open, hair blowing in the wind. As she drove she realized she'd be passing right by the small Emerson Falls grocery store. She pulled her car into the parking lot and headed into the store.

"Hey, Roger," she said to the clerk at the counter as she walked in.

"Hey, Megan," said Roger. "How's it going?"

"Good," she said. "I'm in a rush. Can you point me to any pads of paper you have here?"

"You need some paper? I've also got lined notebooks …" Roger began.

"Sorry, no, just trying to see what you have here."

"Ahh. Working with Officer Coleman again?" Roger said with a wink. By now, it was no secret that Megan had helped solve a number of local mysteries.

"Trying to," Megan said, following Roger down a store aisle.

"Here you go," Roger said, pointing. "There's also the little spiral notebooks at the counter." He looked into the air for a moment, thinking. "Pretty sure that's it." A bell rang, indicating someone else had entered the store. "Let me know if you need anything else!" Roger headed to the front of the store in a slow shuffling jog.

"Thanks, Roger," Megan called out after him, but her attention was already on the paper. She'd seen it immediately: stacks of pads of paper that seemed to be an exact match for what Heather had written on, and what the notes in the parking lot and in Roman's trailer had been written on.

"Drat," Megan said to herself. "And for that matter, the vacation rental could have this paper. Anyone could have bought this paper." She chewed her lip a moment, then walked over toward the health care section. She scanned the shelves until she found what she was looking for: eye drops. "Interesting," Megan said. While the empty space on the shelves indicated that there was room allotted for several boxes of eye drops, only one box remained on the shelf. "Very interesting," she said. "But also, it tells me nothing." Giving up, she headed back toward the front of the store. Lost in thought, she stepped to the side to let Roger pass her, another customer in a dark red T-shirt trailing behind him.

"Hey!"

Megan looked up to see the customer behind Roger smiling at her. Brenden.

"Hey!" she said. "Fancy meeting you here!"

"Ran out of solution for my contacts," Brenden said. "I'm heading out to meet up with my agent and some folks for some more climbing out at Ryan's Wall and thought I'd stop in while I have a chance!"

"You're in the right place," Megan said. "And not just because it's the only store within miles."

"I resemble that remark," Roger said, chuckling. "Find what you need?"

"Yes and no," Megan said. "But thanks for helping me. I'll see you later!"

She tossed a wave to include both Roger and Brenden and soon was back on the road toward Heather's rental. Shortly, she slowed the car for a turn the GPS said was coming up on the right. "Oh, there you are, you sneaky rascal," she said to the dirt road she almost missed, and she turned. Having to drive at a crawl to avoid all the potholes made the road seem even longer than it was, but eventually the road opened to a clearing in which stood a picture perfect cottage by the river. The same little red car Megan had seen Heather get into earlier at Ryan's Wall was parked near the front door.

Exiting her car, Megan immediately heard the familiar shushing of the river, and she smiled. This, she thought, would definitely be a lovely place to return to after a long day of filming. Being Assistant Director apparently had its perks. The haunted hotel was nice enough, but a place of solitude by the rushing water was everything Megan wanted.

"And everything I have," she said to herself, smiling again.

A canopy of trees made the temperature here several degrees cooler than it had been out at the rock wall, and Megan almost wished for a light jacket. Dappled sunlight filtered through and pointed to the absence of trees on the other side of the cottage, where the river passed through wide and strong. Megan stepped up the two wooden stairs that led to a deck that stretched all across the front of the house and around to the side.

Megan knocked on the door and waited. After about thirty seconds, she knocked again and looked for a doorbell. "Maybe she's out back on the deck," Megan said, but she rang the doorbell and waited a while longer. Still no one came.

Megan looked back at the car. She was sure that was the same car Heather had driven earlier in the day. Wasn't it? Megan didn't have much of a memory for cars, but this one looked the same to her. She knocked again.

When still no one answered, Megan walked around the side of the cottage, calling out before her so as not to startle anyone. "Heather?" she said. "Heather, it's Megan. Megan Montaigne. Are you out here?"

She turned the corner onto the sunny deck, fully expecting to see Heather there, sitting on a lounge chair and sipping a glass of red with a plate of cheese, maybe brie, and some high-end crackers. Or as high-end as she could get at Roger's store, anyway.

She had been right about the deck: it was wide and deep, with built-in benches along the wall and several deck chairs positioned strategically to get the best view of the river. The river itself was showing off, flirting with and caressing giant boulders out toward its middle, racing over shallower rocks and sparkling in the sun.

But there was no sign of the sharp dark-haired woman.

Megan thought back to the car again, on the other side of the cottage. Had someone come to pick Heather up? Had she gone for a walk? The sun was so lovely, and it had been a long day. Maybe Heather wouldn't mind if Megan just sat on the deck and took a quick nap …

Megan walked up to the sliding glass door to try one more time. She knocked loudly but carefully—knocking on glass always made her nervous—but Heather didn't appear from this direction either. Finally Megan put a hand up to shield her eyes from the glare as she gazed through the windows, looking for movement. And that's when she saw her.

Heather was lying on the floor, face turned to the side, eyes open, a dark pool growing around her head.

"Oh crap," Megan said.

Heather was dead.

FIFTEEN

"How was she killed? Could you see?" Rae asked.

After notifying Max, answering all the police questions, enduring Max's raised eyebrows about how she seemed to be happening upon a lot of murders lately, and promising not to leave the area, Megan had sent a text to Owen, Lily, Edison, and Rae, telling them to meet at Rae's to discuss the latest developments. Lily, still caught up in her busy day, hadn't yet arrived. But the rest were there, huddled in their favorite corner booth. Rae had brought over a platter of chips, a variety of salsas, and a bottle of their favorite wine, on the house, and now sat perched on the edge of a seat. Her eyes were scanning the room for customers who needed her attention, but her ears were fully engaged in the conversation.

"I couldn't see too far into the cottage, but there was blood all around her head," Megan said. "I mean it's jumping to conclusions to say she was killed, but …"

"But she was killed," Owen said. He dipped a chip in the hottest salsa and took a bite.

"Seems pretty likely," Megan said. She'd been so busy filling everyone in that she'd hardly touched her wine glass. She remedied that now by taking a long sip.

"Okay," Owen said. "So then the question is, who would want Bee, Roman, *and* Heather dead? We're running out of people here."

Megan shook her head. "I really was starting to think it was Heather. But then again, it did seem people either loved her or hated her. Who did she cross? Did she get in someone's way? Did she threaten to reveal something? Or, again, was it just wrong place wrong time?"

"This does seem personal," Edison said. "In her own home. Rental home, but still. In her space."

"So it had to be someone she knew," Megan said. "No signs of forced entry. Then again, it would be easy to trick someone these days. Tell them you're there with a delivery, and next thing you're in the door."

"Did you gather anything else from the police at Heather's?" Owen asked. "Any clues?"

"Not a lot," Megan said. "They were looking at tire tracks but there seemed to be a ton of them. From where I was standing, it didn't look like much had been disturbed in the room. It looked tidy, as you'd expect from Heather."

"Any blunt objects nearby? A fire poke? A lamp?" Rae asked. She twitched, thinking a customer needed her, then settled again when she realized the patron was just heading toward the restrooms.

"I still think Roman's wife is an interesting option. Isn't it always the spouse?" Owen said. "Disgruntled, pissed off that he's not paying the child support, all that?"

"But then why kill Bee and Heather?" Edison asked.

"Well, Bee could have been an accident," Owen said. "Remember the note in Roman's trailer? Someone was trying to lure him to the wall that night."

"The note in Roman's trailer said it was from Fox," Megan said.

"It could have been from someone else, who just signed it from Fox," Owen said.

"But who was the other note for?" Rae said. "The one Megan found in the parking lot? Did they ever figure that out?"

"Or was it a decoy?" Megan said. "I keep thinking about how Fox was there that night. It makes sense that the note to Roman was from him. On the other hand, if the note was from Fox to Roman, why would he send himself a note, too?"

The pub door opened, and a somber group of climbers, cast, and crew from the film walked in, including Fox, Shay, Piper, Jett, and others Megan recognized but didn't know by name.

"Speak of the devils," Owen said quietly.

"Hush now," Megan said. "They're not all devils. Maybe only one of them."

"Don't say anything interesting while I'm gone," Rae said, wagging her finger at her friends as she popped out of her seat to take care of the newly arrived guests.

"Have you asked Fox about that?" Edison said. "Why he was at the gym? Because now's your chance."

"I know he was out on a run," Megan said. "He and Piper had made that clear earlier that afternoon. But they didn't go on their run together, in the end. They had a fight."

"About what?" Owen said, snagging another chip and re-filling his wine glass.

Megan shrugged. "They didn't say. My assumption was relationship issues. Piper wanted more out of the relationship, I think."

"Didn't Fox and Heather hook up?" Owen said.

"Yeah," Megan said, "and so did Heather and Asher. Edison's employee. Speaking of whom, do you know where he went after you guys got back from the wall this morning, Edison?"

"He and I were both with the Low Gravity Gear reps all afternoon," Edison said. "You were already at Heather's before we got out of our meetings."

"Same with Lexi?" Megan said.

"Same with Lexi," Edison said. "Why, do you have reason to suspect her?"

"No," Megan said. "But it's just nice to check someone off the list. Like when you write a to-do list and the first thing on the list is 'write to-do list.' Boom. Done. Anyway, so Asher and Lexi were with you. Where did the other climbers go? After the bus dropped them back at River Rock," Megan asked. She glanced over at the group from the film, trying to read their faces. Did anyone look overly distraught? Like they were faking it? Or underly concerned? Someone told a joke and some others chuckled, but it was all quite subdued. Megan studied Fox. Did he look like a killer?

Her attention shifted to Piper. Piper was sitting next to Fox again. Had they made up? And if so, why? Sure enough, Piper slid a glance toward Fox that seemed to indicate intimacy, a shared secret.

Shay was there, too, head tucked in as she talked quietly with the person next to her. Megan thought it might be the person who had directed her to Roman's trailer, but she wasn't sure. Of all the people, Shay seemed the quietest at the moment. Her body language was tight, arms held close to herself, shoulders slumped.

And then there was Jett. Jett didn't seem to be interacting with the others much. He looked like a man who wanted to be somewhere else. Like he had unfinished business on his mind.

Megan's attention turned back to Shay. Shay made her think of Brenden.

If Brenden was climbing, who was he climbing with?

"Guys," Megan said. "When I was on my way to Heather's, I stopped in at the store. Brenden came in just as I was leaving. He said he was on his way back to Newhalem to do some more climbing. But what if he actually was coming the other direction; what if he'd just been at Heather's?"

"Why would he stop at the store on his way back, then?" Edison said. "That seems unnecessary."

"He said he needed solution for his contacts," Megan said, mind whirling. "You need solution for your contacts regardless of whether you've just murdered someone, I guess?" She paused. "Contact lens solution, which coincidentally is in the same aisle as the eye drops?" She looked again at the table of climbers. "And if he's climbing right now, just who exactly is he climbing with? Everyone is here."

Megan was halfway out of her seat when Edison grabbed her arm. "You're not going without one of us," he said.

"Fine," Megan said. "Come along. But I'm driving."

Owen and Edison popped out of their seats and followed, Edison first grabbing a large envelope that had been sitting on the seat beside him.

"What's that?" Megan said.

"Files from Roman's computer," Edison said. "And email printouts. Stuff I have to go through to figure out where everything stands in financing this film. Although at this point …"

Megan shook her head. She didn't envy Edison, all the hard decisions he was going to have to make and conversations he might have to have.

As they passed Rae on their way out, Megan yelled over her shoulder, "I'll call you later!"

"You'd better!" Rae called back.

The threesome piled into Megan's car, Owen in back and Edison riding shotgun.

"What, exactly, are we hoping to find?" Owen said, leaning

forward to stick his head between the front seats. His ability to remain calm even in chaos was epic.

"Is your seatbelt on?" Megan said. She didn't wait for a reply but peeled out of Rae's parking lot and turned the car down Highway 20.

Owen sat back and belted up. "What are we hoping to find?" he repeated.

"I want to know if Brenden is actually where he said he was going to be." She turned her head toward Edison without her eyes leaving the road. "Or if he's even skipped town. Can you call Sidney and see if Brenden has checked out?"

Edison took out his phone and tapped out a text. "Remington doesn't answer his phone," he explained. "But he'll text back."

The twenty-minute drive ahead of them seemed like it would take hours. The three sat in tense silence for a while, then Edison pulled out the papers from the envelope. "Sorry, you don't mind if I get some work done? It's just that it's all crazy and …"

"No problem," Megan said. She was too lost in thought for conversation anyway. If only she'd stopped to talk to Brenden at the store, she thought. She tried to remember what his clothes looked like. Had there been blood? Was he even there to get contact solution? Or was he there to get bleach to clean up after himself? To clean his car? Had he bought fresh clothes so he could dump what he'd worn to the crime scene?

"Anything interesting?" Owen said casually to Edison as Edison continued to read.

"Contracts, contracts, contracts …" Edison murmured. He put the papers down. "It's a crime, really, that kids in high school don't learn how to read contracts. Everyone needs to know how to read contracts, but who ever learns? Just my two cents." He picked up the papers and dug back in. Within a minute, though, he put them down again to check his phone, which was buzzing with an incoming text.

"Remington says Brenden hasn't checked out yet," Edison said, putting his phone away.

"Isn't that, like, privileged information? Privacy and such?" Owen said. "Is he allowed to tell you that?"

"Sidney and Edison are very privileged," Megan said over her shoulder.

"True, I suppose," Edison said. "But you did ask me to find out."

"I'm willing to exploit your privilege when it helps me," Megan said, grinning.

They flew along the highway, the Skagit River alongside them dipping nearer and further from the road and racing in the opposite direction. Megan could hardly keep to the lower speed limit as she snailed the car through Marblemount before taking the hard left that finally led them officially into the North Cascades National Park.

"Fifth least-visited national park," Owen said casually. "Don't tell anyone about it, please. I'd like if we could keep it to ourselves."

"Selfish," Megan said, but she agreed. Relative to the other national parks, North Cascades National Park was difficult to get to. And that was fine with her. Let the mobs go to Great Smoky Mountains and the Grand Canyon and Yellowstone. She was perfectly happy to savor the pristine mountain scenery all by herself.

As they neared Ryan's Wall near Newhalem, Megan's phone, attached to her dashboard with a magnet, vibrated with a text. "Looks like it's from Lily," Megan said, but she didn't take her hands off the wheels. They were almost to their destination, and Megan would check her messages there.

Finally, they reached the crag. Edison folded the email printouts and slipped them into his pocket while Megan pulled the car onto a small strip of parking area off the side of the road.

There were two other cars there. The trio raced out of the car, trying not to trip over rocks on the approach to the wall.

"Do you see him?" Megan said, looking up at the rock face. This was not a bouldering wall. He wouldn't be up there alone. She didn't know what kind of car Brenden was driving, and didn't recognize either car, regardless.

The scraggly trees obscured their vision but finally Edison pointed. "There, two thirds up the wall. Isn't that him?"

"Who's with him, then?" Megan said. She remembered Lily's text, and pulled her phone out of her pocket.

Sorry I couldn't make it on time! Lily wrote. *At Rae's now. She told me you raced off.*

Yes, Megan typed back, trying not to stumble as she texted and walked over rocks at the same time. *At the wall now, looking for Brenden.*

Any news on Heather? Lily wrote.

Nothing new yet, Megan answered.

My colleague said Heather was staying at the cottage with a guy, Lily wrote. *Have they talked to him?*

Megan stopped cold. *What guy? Do you have a name?*

Owen and Edison stopped, too, eyes on Megan. "What's up?" Owen said.

I don't know, Lily texted. *Will find out, hang on.*

"Lily says Heather was renting the cottage with someone else. A man," Megan said.

"Who?" Edison said.

"I don't know yet," Megan said. "She's asking."

The person at the base of the wall, who was belaying Brenden, turned as he heard Megan, Edison, and Owen approaching. It was Troy.

"Oh, that's right," Megan said under her breath, slightly embarrassed. Brenden had said he was meeting his agent out at the wall. "Congratulations, Megan, you've won the Gold Medal in Jumping to Conclusions."

"What?" said Edison.

"Nothing, nothing," said Megan. "Hey, Troy," she called out.

"Megan," Troy said. "Edison. And …?"

"Owen," said Owen. "I'd shake hands but I don't want you to drop Brenden," he laughed.

"You guys out to do some climbing again?" Troy said, eyeing their street clothes. "Gear in the car?"

Troy's attention shifted quickly as Brenden yelled suddenly, having nearly slipped.

"Oh gosh," Megan said, her hand rushing to cover her heart. "That scared me!"

"It's safer than it seems, if you're taking precautions," Troy said, keeping a careful eye on Brenden. "That's why we have all the safety equipment."

"So you've been climbing a while yourself?" Megan asked. Her eyes were also glued to the climber. He was so far above them, it almost hurt her neck to look up from the base of the rock. He moved with the grace she'd seen in the gym, but outside on the rocks it seemed both so much more beautiful and so much more dangerous. Uncontrolled. Primal.

"I'm not an expert by any means," Troy said, but something about the way he said it made it sound like he was just trying to come across as humble. "But hanging around these guys has really shown me how it can be done. Shown me the ropes," he said, laughing at his own joke.

Megan tossed a glance at Edison, who smiled back. "Yeah, it's definitely inspiring," she said. "Pretty sure I'm going to have to get myself a membership at River Rock. I hear the owner is all right."

Edison grinned.

"So you guys are just out here …?" Megan said to Troy, leaving the sentence open.

"I'm heading back to LA soon. Just wanted to spend a little more time with my client while I have the chance. Get some pointers," Troy said. The rope he held was tight so he pulled the rope through the belay device to give Brenden more slack to climb with. "Maybe I'll star in a film myself some day," he said with a quick wink at Megan.

"That would be fun," Megan said, not sure what to say. "Okay, well, we just were … uh … driving by and thought we'd stop." She cringed at the transparency of her own lie, but didn't bother to think of something better. She called up to Brenden. "Stay safe, Brenden!" she said.

The trio were quiet as they left the wall, but as soon as she thought they were out of earshot, Megan sighed. "I really thought I had something there," she said.

"Hey, never hurts to follow an instinct," Edison said, putting a reassuring hand on her shoulder.

As they drove back toward Emerson Falls, Edison started digging back into the emails. "So much paperwork," he grumbled, eyes scanning the pages.

"Will you keep filming, Edison?" Owen said, straining forward from within his seatbelt in the back. "Seems like it's a cursed set or something. Is it worth it?"

Edison sighed and shook his head. "At this point so much has gone into it … I mean, it's business. I'm not saying I'm not torn. I definitely am. Three lives …" He looked at the stack of papers in his hands. "But so many other lives would be affected if we pulled the plug. There's not really a 'win' in this situation. But we could create so much more loss. These people who are relying on this job for their rent, their mortgages, their kids' schools …" He shook his head again and put his eyes back on the emails, immediately absorbed again.

"It's really difficult," Megan said sympathetically. "I'm glad I'm not in your shoes. But I know whatever decision you make will be the right one."

She pulled the car into Rae's parking lot. She and Owen got out of the car, but Edison was deep in the emails and hardly noticed they'd stopped.

"See you inside?" Megan said to Edison, then she shut the car door behind her.

Immediately on entering, Megan saw Lily waving at her from the corner booth, sitting there with Max.

"Hey!" said Lily as she shifted to make room for the others. "Find anything out?"

"False alarm," Megan said as she sat next to Lily. "I thought I was onto something, but …"

"It happens," Max said. "To the best of us. Can I buy you a drink?"

"Lemon drop, please," Megan said. "And keep 'em coming. What about you guys? Did you discover anything? What's the status on Heather?"

Rae slid over already carrying a lemon drop and overheard the question. "Word on the street is blunt force trauma to the head. Fingerprints wiped off the suspected murder weapon, a wrought iron candlestick."

"Already you know everything! Will you ever reveal your sources, Rae?" Lily said, laughing, her crystalline voice ringing like angels.

Rae looked at Max and winked. "Never," she said.

"Wait, is your source Max?" Megan said, shocked.

Max put his hands up in front of him. "No, no, no, no!" he laughed. "Not me! And I don't know who her source is, either."

"But she's right?" Owen said. "Professor Plum, in the river cottage, with a candlestick. Interesting."

A sudden and familiar stream of light heralded the opening

of the restaurant door, and in the beam of light stood Edison. The emails were in his hand, and the look on his face spelled trouble.

"What's up, Edison?" Megan said, as the whole crew once again shuffled in their seats to make room for one more. "You look disturbed."

"I have a mess to clean up," he said. "And I'm going to have to figure out a very diplomatic way to do it. What's more, I really could use Heather or Roman's help, but … Anyway. If I'm reading these emails right, Low Gravity Gear apparently gave bonus money to the actors, but not all of the actors may have gotten it."

"What do you mean?" asked Max.

"Emails between Roman and Troy. Roman complaining that the money was meant for Brenden, and that he was going to have to tell the climbers," Edison said. "I don't know if Brenden knows. I suspect he's not going to be very excited about it."

"Troy!" Lily said. "I almost forgot. That's who was staying at the cottage with Heather. A guy named Troy."

All heads turned to Lily.

"Troy Langley?" she said, shrinking back a bit at all the sudden attention. "What? Wrong person?"

"Troy, the agent?" Megan said. "Troy was staying with Heather?" She turned to Edison. "Were they dating?"

"I have no idea," Edison said, flustered. "I didn't know. I thought she'd hooked up with Fox, though?"

"And Asher?" Megan said. "But if she was dating someone, and she hooked up with Fox and Asher … I can't see as that would make a boyfriend particularly happy." She shivered involuntarily and rose to her feet, lemon drop untouched. "We need to get back to the wall."

"Do you think they're still there?" Owen said, racing after her, followed by all the others.

"We have to try." She swooped into her car, all her focus on the rock climbing area that now seemed hundreds of miles away. She waited just a moment to let Max get on the road before her, in which time Edison, Owen, and Lily barely made it into her car before she raced away after him out Highway 20 toward Newhalem.

The adrenalin in the car was almost palpable. Megan wove through the details of the mystery out loud as she drove. "Troy. Brenden's agent. He must have held the money back and not told Brenden. Caitlyn and Georgia both told me how much Roman loved the climbers. He must have been threatening to tell Brenden about the money. So Troy killed Roman. Then … then he killed Heather to clean it all up."

"And out of jealousy, maybe," Owen contributed. "But why did he kill Bee?"

"Bee may have just been an accident," Megan said, eyebrows furrowed in concentration. "Heather could have helped with that. Remember, Edison, how Heather finagled her way into your office via Asher?"

"I just remembered something, too," Lily said. "Remember when I said I thought Troy looked familiar? I saw him at the grocery store. I was in the health care section getting some things to update my first aid kits. He was there, too."

"By any chance was he buying eye drops?" Megan said, her eyes catching Lily's in the back seat through the rear-view mirror."

"I wasn't paying close attention. But that absolutely could have been where he was in the store. By the eye drops." She nodded slowly at the memory in her mind.

Megan followed behind Max, who was speeding toward the wall, but her deeply instilled lawfulness kept her from driving quite as fast as he was. After not too long he was out of sight.

"He knows where the wall is, right?" Owen said.

"He was there this morning, remember?" Megan said. Still,

she wished she could have been in his car with him.

Finally, just past Newhalem, Megan pulled her car in behind Max's on the side of the road. One of the other cars they'd seen before had left, but one remained.

"Was there anyone else here when we were here earlier?" Megan yelled over her shoulder to Edison as they all raced to the wall. "I thought one of those cars was Brenden's and one was Troy's, but …?"

Edison didn't answer but kept jogging.

When they arrived at the wall, they could see Max talking to someone who was waving his arms wildly.

"That's Troy," Megan said. Panicked, she looked around the wall and the rocks below for evidence of Brenden. "Did he kill Brenden, too?"

When they could finally hear the conversation Max and Troy were having, Troy was protesting vociferously. What's more, his pants were ripped and covered in blood, and he was standing awkwardly, favoring one leg.

"I didn't know!" Troy said, and suddenly it was clear he was sobbing. "I didn't kill her! I didn't know! I was with that girl Caitlyn all afternoon, and then Brenden asked me to come out here with him! I fell and he went for help!"

Megan's mouth dropped. Brenden? Sweet Brenden? He couldn't be the murderer. Could he? She started putting puzzle pieces together in her mind. Bee was gone because Brenden wanted the lead role. Roman must have been reconsidering whether to cast Brenden in the lead. Heather had gotten in the way. Or had helped, and knew too much.

"There was a car here earlier that isn't here now," Edison offered.

"That was his!" Troy said. "He said he was going to get me help, but now that you say Heather is dead …" He started sobbing again.

"Where do you think he's gone, then?" Max said.

Troy shrugged helplessly. "His hotel?" he cried. "Then the first flight out. Oh, Heather!"

Max took a few steps away and called for an ambulance. He then requested that an officer be sent to the resort to look for Brenden, and detain him.

"How did you get hurt?" Megan asked, pointing to Troy's pants.

Troy looked down like he had forgotten he was hurt. "I was up on the wall, and Brenden was belaying me. I slipped. I'm not a great climber. I fell, and he didn't catch me." He shook his head. "It doesn't make sense. He's a pro. He acted like it was an accident but he's too good for that. I think it was intentional."

"How far did you fall?" Megan said, wincing.

"Apparently not as far as he'd been hoping," Troy said. "I caught a hold on my way down, and slipped again, but it slowed my fall just enough, I guess." He shifted his weight and sat down on a large boulder nearby.

"Ambulance is on the way," Max said.

"I think I can make it to your car, if that would be quicker," Troy said. He stood and gingerly put weight on his hurt leg. "In fact, it's my left leg. I hate to leave the rental car out here. I'm sure I can drive."

"Well, we can head to the road and meet the ambulance," Max said. "But probably they should take care of you."

Max stepped close to Troy. "I'll help you walk," he said, and Troy draped his left arm over Max's shoulder. Owen jogged over to help on Troy's other side. They stumbled slowly back toward the road.

Megan stood for a moment, looking at the base of the wall, while Lily followed after the others.

"You coming?" Edison said to Megan.

Megan put up a finger. "Something's not right," she said. She started walking toward the wall.

"Megan?" Edison said. He looked back toward Max and the others, then turned and jogged toward Megan.

"What is it?" he said when he reached her.

"Over there by those rocks," Megan said, pointing. "See that dark red? That's clothes. That's not rocks." She started walking faster toward the red object, picking her way among the boulders.

"Did you hear that?" she said.

"Hear what?" Edison said.

"A groan," she said. "I'm sure of it."

As they got closer to the red object, it became clear. The dark red object was a T-shirt, and there was a person inside it.

"Brenden!" Megan said, running the last few yards. She stopped before touching him. "He's bleeding," she said, pointing to his head. Blood had spilled out onto the rock beneath him. "Oh, Brenden!" Megan said. She gently reached for his wrist to feel for a pulse, expecting to find nothing. But suddenly she gasped.

"Call Max," she said. "Get Max now. Don't let them leave. Brenden is alive."

SIXTEEN

"I cannot believe you people talked me into this," Rae grumbled. She was only about two feet off the ground and clinging for dear life to the giant yellow jug-like holds of a V0 route, but the way Rae was complaining a person couldn't be blamed for thinking she was at the top of the wall with no way down. Nonetheless, she had everyone laughing. As a way for them to blow off steam, Edison had opened up the gym just for a few people, and the group had convinced Rae that it was her duty to Edison and to Emerson Falls to give climbing a try.

"Just wait until we get you in a harness, Rae!" Owen called out. This was a friendly, stress-free afternoon and they were taking it easy—meaning everyone else was sitting or lying down on the soft, deeply cushioned gray floor, talking with each other and shouting out occasional encouragements to whoever might actually be climbing at the moment.

"You're doing great, Rae," Brenden said. "You've got this. Right hand can go to that hold about a foot away from where it is right now. Trust yourself, don't talk yourself into your fear. You've got this."

"Only person in the whole gym being nice to me," Rae muttered. She stared at the hold Brenden had suggested for a while, as if she could will it to come closer to her rather than her having to reach for it. Finally, she lunged forward to grab it. Success.

"Nice!" Brenden said. "We'll get you into the competitions yet."

Megan laughed. "You're too kind to her," she said. She tapped her own head where Brenden had suffered his injury. "How's the skull?"

Brenden touched the bandage wrapped around his head. "I guess I'm lucky Troy just hit me with a rock, instead of dropping me while I was way up the wall," he said. "I'm doing okay. They're going to keep watch for signs of danger, but," he shrugged. "I've probably had worse."

"So, Max, what, exactly, was the full story?" Owen said. "I haven't heard yet and Rae, here, has been too busy free soloing this wall to tell me everything she heard from her secret sources."

"I can hear you," Rae said over her shoulder. "I'm right here."

"Keep climbing, Rae!" Lily called out with enthusiasm. "You're doing amazing!" Next to her on the mat was her husband, Steve, his curly salt-and-pepper hair a mop that almost rivaled Owen's. They'd decided that on this special occasion both of them could afford to leave the B&B for a while. They had left a friend's teenaged daughter in charge, with permission to call them for any emergency. Lily reached for Steve's hand and grinned at him.

"The best I've ever seen you climb, Rae," Steve said. He pushed his wire-rimmed glasses up the bridge of his nose and smiled back at his wife. She giggled and leaned into him fondly.

Rae lifted her left foot and moved it to a hold slightly up and to the right from where it had been. "Never again," she murmured.

"And yet she won't stop," Owen said.

Owen's boyfriend, Parker, had also joined them. "You guys are so mean to poor Rae," Parker said. He lay down on the mat, knees up, and stretched. Owen reached over and ruffled Parker's short blond hair.

"Listen to your boyfriend," Rae said. She moved her left hand to another hold, then quickly moved her right foot.

"You are a natural, Rae!" Edison said. "I'll get your membership papers started!"

"Well," said Max, returning to Owen's question. "Megan had most of the story figured out already. Would you like to recap, Megan?"

Megan's long hair had come loose from her ponytail while climbing. As she thought about where to start she pulled her hair out of the elastic, smoothed her hair with her hands, and then put the elastic back on. "Okay. So, originally the only target was Roman. The other murders were just unfortunate dominos that were knocked down along the way."

"'Unfortunate Dominos' is the name of my new band," Owen said. Parker chuckled.

Megan continued. "Let's start with Heather. All of this was Troy's idea. But he convinced his girlfriend—Heather—to go along with him. Heather hadn't had an easy life, and it sounds like she had run across more than one manipulative person in her past. Troy fit right in. She had a complicated perspective of what love was, and maybe hadn't yet figured out how to set boundaries with a partner. Anyway, Troy manipulated her. People always said Heather could do anything, and that was true—including figuring out how to turn off the security camera system, and how to sabotage a speed climbing wall.

"We now know that Fox had challenged Roman to a speed climbing competition, but they hadn't set a time. Heather overheard this conversation and told Troy, just casually. Troy wrote notes to Fox and Roman, which are the notes we saw. Each of them saw the note they got and thought it was from the other—that is, Fox thought his was from Roman, and Roman thought his was from Fox. They texted each other to arrange a time, neither questioning whether the other had actually sent the initial note. Fox had a fight with Piper that night, though, and he was late. Roman got there on time. But Bee, completely unaware of all of this, had decided to work on his climbing skills. He was competitive and wanted to improve. When Roman got there, Bee was already dead. When Fox ran by, Roman was long gone."

"But why didn't Fox tell the police that?" Owen said.

"Because it looked suspicious," Max said. "People don't only hide things because they are guilty. Often they hide things because they worry they'll look guilty, even if they aren't."

"Exactly," said Megan. "And Fox told me he was going on a run because it was true; he was going to run to the gym. But he didn't tell me he was meeting Roman to climb the wall, because they weren't supposed to be there, technically, but Roman had said it would be okay, as he had access. So that was Bee. An intentional death but not the intended victim. But it actually was convenient for Troy and Heather because it threw everyone off their trail. No one could figure out the motive, and it threw other suspects into the mix."

"Like me, for example," Brenden said. "Brenden Kogut, trying to further his career by killing the competition. That didn't feel great."

"I'm sure not," Lily said.

Megan frowned. Brenden had been through so much, and it turned out he was a stellar human being. She felt bad for having ever suspected him but that was the nature of detective work. She sighed and continued with her narrative. "So next, Roman. Troy's reason for wanting to kill Roman is that Roman was going to tell Brenden about the money Low Gravity Gear had given Troy, that was meant to be passed along to Brenden.

Because Troy was Brenden's agent, the agreement and money went through Troy. Brenden never knew he hadn't gotten all the money he was supposed to get. They've been digging into it and it seems this isn't the first time Troy has skimmed some money off the top that was meant for his clients. Anyway, as we know, Roman loved the climbers. Everyone kept telling us that."

"More than his own family," Lily said.

Brenden looked down, shaking his head.

"Roman wanted so much to be a part of the climbers' inner circle," Megan continued. "He wrote this movie because of that desire, and when he found out Troy was withholding cash meant for Brenden, of course he was going to say something. It might not even have come into play except that when Bee died, negotiations began to get Brenden into the lead role. Suddenly Troy's deception came to light and everything was about to be exposed."

"So Troy fed Roman eye drops?" Steve asked.

"Troy bought the eye drops the day Lily saw him at Roger's store. But he relied on Heather, once again. Heather knew Roman liked to go for runs, and there was a sweet crew member who always put lemonade in his trailer for him to drink when he came back. Heather knew that, too. She watched him, and watched for the woman who delivered the lemonade. Roman didn't lock his trailer because he didn't keep much in there. And, I suppose, because he figured this is Emerson Falls, and what could happen here? Once the lemonade was in the trailer, Heather slipped in and dumped four bottles of eye drops into the drink. He wasn't expected anywhere, so he died before he was missed. And that was the end of Roman."

"Harsh way to go. Eye drops. Who knew?" said Parker.

"I am never drinking anything any of you serve me again," said Max. "Except you, Rae."

While Megan had been talking, Rae had downclimbed the

yellow route. Creaking and groaning, she now joined the others on the floor.

"I would never hurt you, Max," Rae said. "You're my favorite."

"I thought I was your favorite, Rae?" Brenden joked.

Rae shook her head, smiling.

"Okay, then Heather," Lily said sadly. "I think I can guess where this is going."

"You probably can," said Megan. "First there was the fact that Heather knew everything and was involved in everything. She was probably involved in even more that we don't know about yet. But second, Heather was starting to stray. Her liaisons with Fox and Asher weren't just part of the scheme. She was legitimately restless, and starting to look elsewhere. Troy saw this and was jealous and angry. Tale as old as time. Enraged man kills woman. Since they were staying together in an isolated cottage, he had easy access." Megan paused. "And then, that brings us to Brenden."

"The survivor," Lily said with a smile at the climber.

"After he killed Heather, Troy called Brenden to go climbing. Brenden was the last loose end. I'm not sure if Troy had an exact plan for how he was going to kill Brenden, but climbing outside offers lots of opportunities for 'accidents.' Still, Brenden is too good of a climber. If Troy was counting on Brenden to fall, he should have had a plan B. Or rather, I guess a rock to the back of the head *was* his plan B."

"If you guys hadn't come out when you did, I don't know what would have happened," Brenden said. "Thanks."

"I'd say 'anytime,'" Megan said, "but instead I'll go with 'hopefully never again.' Anyway, that's pretty much that."

"Troy's been surprisingly talkative," Max said. "Bit of a narcissist. Or maybe a sociopath. They tend not to be able to see that they've done anything wrong."

"And you've decided to stop film production for now, Edison?" Lily said. "I'm sure that was a tough decision."

"Yeah. For now, anyway," Edison said. He dusted some chalk off his shirt. "I talked with Jett and we agreed we need to take some time to reassess. Too much water under the bridge to just keep going forward. He has some ideas on how to improve the script, and he says he knows a great screenwriter who can help. I've sent each of the cast and crew home with a bonus to try to make up for it. We'll reconvene soon, but for now, we just need some time."

"And Brenden?" said Megan. "What's next for you?"

"Aside from being Rae's personal coach?" Brenden said.

Rae turned her head. "I think I might adopt you. Only person in this whole town who's been nice to me."

Brenden laughed. Megan thought how good it was to see him laugh so freely and heartily. He'd had a cloud over him from the day she met him. Now it was gone.

"I've been dirtbagging out of an old van," Brenden said. "With the bonus money from Edison and Low Gravity Gear, I'm hoping I can soup it up a bit. Install a nice kitchen area, maybe, some general improvements to make it nicer. Especially since Shay is going to be joining me for a bit." He paused and smiled lightly to himself. "I suppose we'll go climb until Edison and Jett call us back."

"And maybe I'll join you," Rae said, getting up off the floor with a grunt. "But you've got to help me get to the top of this wall first. And make sure I don't fall."

"If you never fall, you're not trying hard enough," Brenden said. But he got up and went over to help Rae, wearing a huge grin of contentment.

"Truer words never spoken," Megan said. She studied the walls for a moment before deciding on a green route that seemed just a little bit outside of her comfort zone, and she started to climb.

THE MEGAN MONTAIGNE MYSTERIES

For Megan Montaigne, library director, living in the top floor of the mansion-turned-library is a dream come true. At least it was, before the murders started.

"Superb writing, extraordinary characters. A fantastically well-written novel with characters so real that one might reach out and touch them."

"I loved every page of this novel. Did not want to stop reading and wanted more as I read the last word."

DEATH AT GLACIER LAKE

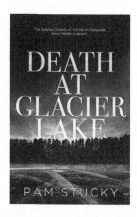

A fast-paced, atmospheric mystery that will keep you guessing until the end!

For two decades, the lush, isolated forests of the North Cascades have hidden a secret. Now, twenty years later, a mysterious contest has brought Mindy Harris back to the area she thought she'd left behind forever. A seemingly innocent creative design firm shows up for a company retreat, but all goes awry when one of their own turns up dead. Was it an accident? Murder? And how does the unsolved mystery from twenty years ago play into it all?

"One of the best Kindle books I have read so far. An unusual ending, love and hate, trust and mistrust, a little of everything. Just like real life. Not a cliff hanger, just a good, stand alone story. Loved every bit of it."

"A neat little mystery with the rare virtue that the setting and characters are as interesting as the unfolding story."

More by Pam Stucky

The Balky Point Adventures (MG/YA sci-fi)

"Aliens, infinite universes, ghosts AND time travel ... a winning literary combination if ever there was one." — *Just One More Chapter reviews*

This smart and unforgettable middle grade / young adult science fiction adventure series takes teens Emma, Charlie, Eve, and Ben, along with brilliant but quirky Dr. Waldo and a host of others, on adventures through time and space. Inspired the timeless wonder and fantasy of *A Wrinkle in Time*, with just a dash of *Doctor Who*, the Balky Point Adventures are for readers of all ages who love a good romp through the imaginative marvels of the universes, delivered with heart and wonder. Exciting and imaginative, courageous and thought-provoking, this series commends the strength of compassion, and the inherent power within each person to change the world ... or the universe.

Includes: *The Universes Inside the Lighthouse, The Secret of the Dark Galaxy Stone, The Planet of the Memory Thieves,* and *The Perils of the Infinite Task.*

The Wishing Rock series (contemporary fiction)

"It was just what the doctor ordered, fresh, quirky, funny in places and seasoned with wisdom. Light without being frivolous, it follows the story of a woman trying to find someone to fill her desire for true love and family." — *Tahlia Newland, author*

The Wishing Rock books take readers to the fictional town of Wishing Rock, Washington, on Dogwinkle Island—where all the town's residents live in the same building. In this *Northern Exposure*-esque slice-of-life series, letters between the neighbors and their friends chronicle the twists and turns of the characters' daily lives, and are interspersed with recipes tried and tested by the characters themselves. These novels, filled with wit, wisdom, and recipes, take characters on adventures far and near, and ultimately offer up insightful exploration of the ideas of community, relationships, happiness, hope, forgiveness, risk, trust, and love.

Includes: *Letters from Wishing Rock*, *The Wishing Rock Theory of Life*, and *The Tides of Wishing Rock* (all novels with recipes); *From the Wishing Rock Kitchens: Recipes from the Series* completes the series, with a compilation of all the recipes in the first three books.

The Pam on the Map series (travelogues)

"I couldn't resist reading the entire book, both for the wit and chuckles that I found on nearly every page, and to make sure I didn't miss any of the useful tips that were scattered throughout. I'm big on pre-trip research, and I found some tips in this book that I haven't seen elsewhere." — Emily, Amazon reader

In her Pam on the Map series, Pam sets out to discover and connect with people and places, and to take readers along on her adventures through her almost real-time reports. Raw and real, Pam's tales are infused with candid honesty, humorous observations, and perceptive insights. Pam's descriptive, entertaining, conversational style brings her trips alive, making readers feel as though they're traveling right along with her.

Though they're not guidebooks, the Pam on the Map books are still informative and illuminating, providing useful tips and plentiful ideas for people who might want to follow along in Pam's footsteps.

Includes: *Pam on the Map: Iceland, Pam on the Map: Seattle Day Trips, Pam on the Map (Retrospective): Ireland*, and *Pam on the Map (Retrospective): Switzerland*.

AUTHOR'S NOTE

You should try bouldering!

Dear reader, I want you to know: it is extremely difficult to intentionally kill a specific person in climbing or bouldering! So difficult, in fact, that I had to take some liberties to make this story work. For this, I apologize to my fellow climbers.

I started bouldering in January 2019, and it was like finding magic. (In our 2020 COVID-19 quarantine, bouldering and my climbing gym are among the things I miss most.)

As a writer, I often shape my stories around familiar spaces and ideas; therefore, soon after I started bouldering it occurred to me that I wanted to write a Megan Montaigne mystery with bouldering and/or rock climbing in it.

This is the important part: it is super duper safe to climb in a gym! Not that you can't get hurt; it does happen. But they take safety *very* seriously. I don't want this book to discourage anyone from trying bouldering. Bouldering is amazing. It's good for strength, balance, flexibility, and more. When you're on the wall you can't be thinking about your problems because you've got to be thinking about the holds, your hands, your feet, where you're moving next. What's more, the climbing community is fantastic, and climbing with friends is soul-filling. I've had some of my best, deepest, most vulnerable conversations sitting on the bouldering room floor. When you're literally trying and failing the whole time you're there, and getting yourself up again and trying again, I mean, what better metaphor is there for a life well lived?

So even though I chose to kill someone off in a gym, don't let that deter you. If you're intrigued, go to your local climbing gym and ask them to show you the ropes—or the non-ropes, as it were. Climb on!

ACKNOWLEDGMENTS

I started writing this book shortly before quarantine began for the 2020 COVID-19 pandemic, and finished when my city was just entering Phase 1.5 to exit lockdown. Focus did not always come easy. Writing did not always come easy.

But every day as I tried to write, tens or hundreds of thousands of brilliant, caring, hard-working scientists, doctors, nurses, grocery store clerks, sanitation workers, first responders, mail carriers, delivery people, restaurant workers, and all the other "essential workers" were going out into a scary world and doing their jobs, trying to come up with a vaccine and treatments, saving and healing lives, delivering the foods and goods we needed, keeping the rest of us safe and fed and stocked up on wine and other essentials as we hunkered down to wait out the virus.

I had the luxury of staying home to write because these people put their lives on the line for all of the rest of us. Thank you to all of them, from the bottom of my heart.

CONNECT

If you loved this book, tell your friends and let Pam know! Leave a review online, send a tweet to @pamstucky, and/or drop Pam a note at facebook.com/pamstuckyauthor.

Stay tuned for more! Be among the first to know when a new story is coming out by signing up for Pam's mailing list at pamstucky.com!

Visit pamstucky.com to find out more about Pam and her other fiction and non-fiction books.

Made in the USA
Monee, IL
05 July 2020